Two Loves, One Heart

CARRIE J. KEATON

ISBN
978-1-957895-06-2 (Paperback)
978-1-957895-05-5 (eBook)

Table of Contents

Chapter

ONE

I felt like I was on top of the world.... I, Lynnette Thomas, was now Mrs. William Matthews. We had the most beautiful lawn ceremony. My eyes swept over our guests who had been a part of the most wonderful day of my life.... my wedding ceremony. Smiling happily and gazing over the crowd, I could see that everyone was clearly enjoying themselves.... eating, laughing, talking, and drinking. The clamor from everyone talking and the laughter seemed to fade into the background, as my mind entered a portal in time when Billy and I first became acquainted. Billy had been such a bully when we were growing up. He was two years older than I, and he had picked on me terribly throughout grade school. He used to chase many of the girls and me with frogs and beetles. Billy also jerked my ponytails all the time and always seemed to laugh himself into oblivion at the way I dressed. It was hilarious to him that my mom made me wear tights under my dresses and skirts. As we grew older, Billy began shedding that bullying personality of his and started to see me in a different light. I had blossomed into a very beautiful young woman by the time I had reached my high school years. Many of the girls in my class and on the high school campus envied me. Mother Nature had lavishly given me a graceful figure. The junior and senior girls allowed their jealousy to cause them to be very nasty toward me. Of course, I had nothing to do with attaining the figure God had blessed me with. Even though I possessed a meek and humble attitude and personality, they all still resented me.

By my tenth grade year of high school, I had grown to like Billy. He had gotten a very attentive and generous character that I admired greatly. Billy had turned into an admirable young man that I now really cared for deeply. He walked me to all of my classes and carried my books, and he also carried my lunch tray in the cafeteria at lunchtime. He'd sneak up from behind and sweep me off my feet.... literally, and we would steal sweet, tender kisses.

Billy had a wonderful build and was a football jock. As tall and as handsome as he was, he had rippling biceps. The mere sight of him would make any girl feel butterflies in her stomach. He could have definitely given Mr. Universe a run for his money. The other girls at school were green with envy because Billy was with me. They would have given anything to be in my shoes.... to have this hunk of a guy for their very own.

Several months after Billy and I had been dating, he whisked me around a secluded corner at school and we shared the sweetest, most intimate kiss. Billy then pulled off his senior ring and placed it on a gold chain that he'd taken from his jacket pocket. "I want you to be my steady, Lynnie," he said softly. "I love you."

It was then that Billy asked me to be his sweetheart.... forever.

Without hesitation, I said yes, because I realized that I loved him too.

After Billy and I became sweethearts, the girls at school really envied me now. I was Billy's girl now.

"Lynnie!" a voice rang out, jolting me back into reality.

As I turned, my aunt was approaching me. She flung her arms around me and gave me a loving embrace.

"The ceremony was beautiful sweetheart. You look radiant," Aunt Mary said, in a raised tone.

"I hope that Billy and you have a wonderful life together and grace me with many nieces and nephews.

With a mischievous smile, Aunt Mary added, "Let's hope this marriage lasts longer than mine did."

My aunt kissed me lightly on the cheek and with a mumbled goodbye, left in a haste.

I began to feel tears teasing the corners of my eyes. So I turned abruptly and made my way to the living room. Stopping where I would be partially hidden from my guests behind a large cheval mirror, I tried to blink back the tears that had now begun to cascade down both my cheeks. Thoughts of just how happy I really was today consumed me. I had just gotten married to my childhood sweetheart -- the man that I love and one who loves me with all his heart. Billy had so very proudly displayed me on his arm and it made me feel so loved by him. I realized that I was lucky to have his love and devotion.

"What is this," a deep masculine voice said. "What has upset my beautiful wife?"

Startled, I spun around to see a pair of dark, loving eyes gazing at me. Through the teary blur, I could visualize my handsome husband standing just a few feet away, admiring me affectionately.

Billy was picture perfect as he walked over closer to me, with his long, curly, black hair that sweptback and draped over his broad shoulders. When he saw the tears welled in my eyes, his heavy brows creased with concern.

"Lynnie, baby, you should not be looking so sadly on your wedding day," He spoke softly.

"I'm just so happy Billy," I sniffed.

Billy draped his strong arms around me and tenderly

kissed my forehead.

"You've made me the happiest man on earth by becoming my wife Lynnie. I love you very much Mrs. Matthews."

Interrupting our stolen moment, my niece ran in yelling at the top of her voice.

"Aunt Lynnie! It's time to throw the wedding bouquet!" Tara shrieked.

I turned back to the mirror to glance over my appearance.

Well, Mr. Matthews, How do I look?" I said flashing a broad smile.

"Like a picture from a magazine -- absolutely gorgeous my dear," Billy remarked, extending his hand out to me.

Taking Billy's hand, I gathered up my bouquet and rejoined our awaiting guests out on the terrace.

The impatient, single ladies were all gathered in a group, anxiously waiting for the traditional tossing of the bouquet. Glancing over at Billy, I smiled happily, as he shot me a seductive wink and a loving, reassuring smile. Walking over closer to the crowd, I turned my back to them and threw the bouquet over my head. The ladies began screaming and pushing each other. The sight of them scrambling for the bouquet was hilarious. They reminded me of football players shuffling to recover a fumbled pass.

"I got it! I got it!" a voice yelled from within the crowd. As I looked to try to see who had caught the bouquet, Tara made her way through the crowd clutching the bouquet. I stood there smiling and shaking my head at my elated niece's victory. I should have known that Tara would manage to get that bouquet someway -- somehow.

Billy came over to me and took my hand. He whisked me away to a vacant area in the middle of the terrace. Everyone sort of backed off and encircled the two of us. Then the music started to play. It was a familiar tune.... It was our song, *Always* playing.

"May I have this dance Mrs. Matthews?" Billy said slightly bowing while extending his hand out to me. He very lovingly pulled me into his arms and we began dancing slowly to the rhythm of the music. Looking into Billy's intoxicating eyes, I became lost deep within their depths. It was as though the guests no longer existed and that there was only the two of us in our own fantasy world. I could only hear the sensual music, as we glided across the floor. After a few minutes, everyone else joined us on the floor.

* * * * * * * *

Billy and I mingled with our guests for a few more hours because we were happy that they could share in our blessed event. Afterward, we went inside to change clothes. After saying our goodbyes to everyone and thanked them for sharing in our glorious day, we were sent off in a shower of rice, as we ran for our car. Someone had placed a sign on the sides of the convertible that said *"Just Married."* Billy and I waved our final farewells to everyone as we sped away.

Wiggling closer to Billy, I put my arms around his neck and showered him with feathery kisses.

Lynnie, baby, you need to cut that stuff out. You know that I can't concentrate when you are teasing me like that," Bill remarked in a flustered, husky voice.

Realizing that I was getting him all hot and bothered, I stopped teasing him like that. At any rate, I didn't want to cause us to have an accident. Instead, I decided to just lean on Billy's broad shoulders. He cradled me in his arms and kissed me lovingly on the forehead.

* * * * * * * *

The air smelled so sweet and serene on this country road that we traveled. Breathing in the fragrance of honeysuckles and lilacs, my mind drifted away to our new home in Charleston, South Carolina. I thought of how happy we were destined to be there. Billy would be joining Smelter/Phelps Explorations where he would be project engineer/specialist.

I had three years of college under my belt, and I was majoring in Business Administration. I wanted to obtain my masters in that field, but that dream had been put on hold for now. Billy and I had discussed my finishing school and agreed that I would continue my last year of college in about a year. We both had agreed to allow us the opportunity to get married, get our home organized, and give him a chance to become more established in his new job. I really didn't think that it would be hard for me to go back to school and get my degree because I only needed another year of study to have my requirements met. Postponing school just seemed like a wise thing to do until Billy got settled into his job and got some more money saved up. Right now, I will be content just being a homemaker.

* * * * * * *

I had dozed off in a peaceful sleep while I was dreaming of the happy life that lies ahead of us. The three hours had gone by quickly since we'd left our old hometown of Atlanta, Georgia. I was awakened from my slumbering state by gentle nudging.

"Lynnie -- honey -- We're home. Wake up sleepy head," Billy spoke softly.

I sat up as we were pulling into our driveway. Billy stopped the car and got out. He reached back into the car for me, while extending his hand. I grasped his hand as I slid out on his side of the car. Taking in deep breath of the country air, I walked over to the large elm next to the house. I sat on the bench while Billy carried our luggage inside. I sat there and admired the beauty of the sunset. It seemed to have such a calming, tranquil effect on me.

I felt like I was being caressed in nature's loving, peaceful arms.

After taking in the last of the luggage, Billy joined me on the bench.

"It's beautiful out here. I see now why you wanted a suburban home -- it's so peaceful." He remarked.

"Yes -- it is," I replied admirably.

Both of us sat there and watched as the sun slowly slipped away and darkness was claiming our tranquil surroundings.

Billy and I walked slowly up the walk to our new home, hand in hand. We were about to walk up the steps when Billy spun me around into his strong arms and swept me off my feet.

"Not so fast Mrs. Matthews. I'm carrying you across the threshold," Billy spoke in a sensual tone.

With very little effort, he whisked me through the door and with a quick maneuver of his foot, closed it behind us. Billy began teasingly trailing gentle kisses along my neck. His kisses ignited delightfully tingling sensations in me. Standing me on the floor, he continued his love mission of stirring my rising desires.

As we gazed into each other's eyes, there was little need for words. We joined hands and walked into our bedroom. We embraced and engaged in another sensual, slow kiss. Billy's kiss was warm and delicious as his full lips moved over mine, sending waves of passion crashing through my body. We moved our hands over each other's bodies, searching and caressing until our passions had awakened a desperate need in both of us. Billy's mouth never left mine, as he began unbuttoning my blouse. He put one hand inside my bra and gently caressed my right breast. As unbridled desire soared inside me, I gripped him fervently. He undid my bra while tracing tender kisses behind my ear and along my neck.

Again, Billy's mouth hungrily claimed mine. A sigh of exquisite pleasure escaped from my lips, as one of his hands claimed my breast .... one and then the other.

"Oh Billy," I moaned in a sultry tone, wanting him with all my being. His hot, moist mouth captured the hardened tip of one of my breasts. I was now in senseless state of wanting. While having my mouth still held captive, Billy undone the button and zipper on my trousers. They fell to the floor, as he slid his hands all over my body. I seemed to just unconsciously step out of my trousers, as I yielded to Billy's every touch.

Billy laid me on the bed and I watched him quickly undress. He soon joined me in bed, pulling me closer to him. I could now feel his urgency as moans of pleasure escaped from his sensuous lips and as he kissed me with much desperation. His breathing was quickening as the flames of desire were intensifying. I was nearly on the verge of losing control. My body now ached for release that only he could give. Billy covered my slender body with his muscular one. He shifted the lower part of his body as he slid into me. I arched my back and wrapped my legs around his waist, gripping him tighter inside of me. Billy loved me with all his being, as I watched his muscles flexing over me each time he pressed deeper and deeper into me. We rode on the waves of passion as we rocked and reeled, back and forth, pleasure radiating throughout our bodies. I could feel the heat of him burn deep inside mingled with the heat of my own. He pushed us closer and closer until we reached the peak of total and complete fulfillment.

"Ye-esss!" I cried out, sobbing my pleasure as my world exploded in a million passionate pieces.

Billy followed and the deep guttural sound he made echoed through the room as he clutched me closer, driving deeper into me. Shivers of sexual delight tore through both of us, as we fell satiated from the consummation of our love.

"Billy," I whispered. "I love you."

"I love you too." He answered huskily.

Laying my head across his muscular chest, Billy pulled me in snugly against him. I knew then that we were home.

Chapter

TWO

The weekend seemed to quickly pass. I arose early to prepare breakfast for Billy. Today was his first day on his new job and I wanted to send him off on the right foot. I'd put on a pot of coffee, and stepped outside the door to pick up the morning paper. Placing the paper on the kitchen table, I put some bacon and sausages on the griddle. After adjusting the flame under them, I grabbed a cup of coffee and began thumbing through the paper. Returning to the stove, I turned the bacon and sausages.

"Well," I muttered. I believe you guys are almost ready. Time to make toast."

When I started the toast and removed the bacon and sausages from the griddle, I prepared the griddle for eggs. As I was scrambling the eggs, a warm breath breezed across my neck, followed by a gentle kiss.

"Good morning, baby doll," Billy uttered, while encircling his arms around my waist.

He planted another playful kiss on the back of my neck before seating himself at the table.

I served Billy breakfast and poured him coffee, while he glanced over the paper. We chatted as we ate, exchanging plans that we had mapped out for the day.

Billy left for the office, and I threw on a pair of sweats and tackled the kitchen. After cleaning the kitchen, I finish unpacking our belongings. By afternoon I was beat and needed a break. I freshened up, put on a pair of sunglasses, and went for a stroll. Pinehurst/Sheppard Park was less than a quarter of a mile away from our home. Also, there were some beautiful gardens nearby that were two of South Carolina's attractions. The Cypress Gardens and the Magnolia Gardens had a variety of colorful flowers and several lagoons flanked by cypress trees. I had learned that many of these different flowers and trees came from many lands. I lingered and admired the beauty and the fragrances of the many flowers in the gardens, before continuing on to the park. It was a wonderful day out and there was a nice breeze blowing. I enjoyed it all .... everything, until I reached the park entrance.

During my walk in the park, I approached a pond that seemed like somewhat the center focal point in the whole park. There were groups of swans and ducks swimming all about. There was also a foot walk with banisters that arched over the pond from one end to the other. I thought -- now I should really get a great view from there. Making my way to the foot walk, I walked to the highest point and leaned up against the railing. The view was breathtaking. I sighed, as I leaned over the banisters, admiring the reflection in the water that stared back at me. The gentle summer breeze softly rippled the water as it glided over it.

"Serenity," I uttered. "Serenity!"

Absorbed in my own thoughts, I didn't realize that someone had walked up.

"It's lovely out here isn't it," a feminine voice asked.

I spun around in astonishment to see a rather nice looking lady, probably about my age, smiling warmly. Trailing just behind her was another female and a guy. They too looked about my age.

"Hi -- my name is Samantha Ellington," she said, extending her hand. "Lynnette Matthews," I answered smiling, as I shook her hand. "But you can call me Lynnie."

"You can call me Sam," she added, as she leaned up against the railing.

"Now – uh – uh your face looks a little familiar. I think I've seen you before around here. Don't you live on Lakeshore Drive? I saw new people moving in there." Dee said, her face grimacing from the bright sun.

"Yes, I do," I replied. My husband and I just moved here from Atlanta, Georgia.

"Well .... we are all neighbors then. Let me introduce you to your other two neighbors."

We stepped over to where her friends were, throwing breadcrumbs into the water.

"Hey – you guys – this is Lynnette Matthews. Lynnie, this is Deanna Sanders, who we all call Dee. And this fellow here is her husband Greg."

"Nice to meet you Lynnie," they responded harmoniously.

While shaking both their hands, I just happened to glance at my watch. I hadn't noticed that so much time had slipped by. I knew that I had to go home and fix supper for Billy and me.

"It was really nice meeting all of you, but I've got to get going," I replied anxiously. "It's getting late and my husband Billy will be home soon."

"Hey .... we're on our way home too. Would you mind if we walked back with you?" Dee said. "We can chat on the way."

I agreed, and we laughed, talked, and joked all the way home. They were good people and I was enjoying their company. When we reached my house, we said our goodbyes and I promised to have lunch with them tomorrow.

I went inside and began preparations for supper. After starting supper, I finished the rest of the unpacking. I felt relieved when I put away the last item.

"Thank goodness I'm finished," I uttered.

Making my way back to the kitchen, I checked on supper. Since supper was almost ready, I began setting the table. I knew that Billy would be arriving at any minute. Just as I put the last fork in place, I heard the front door closing.

"Lynnie honey, I'm home."

I stepped into the living room, as Billy was crashing on the sofa.

"Rough day baby?" I asked with sincere concern.

"Yeah -- I'm beat," he groaned.

"I bet that I have a remedy for that," I said with a mischievous wink.

"You just rest right there for a little while. Dr. Matthews will take real good care of you."

I went to the bathroom and drew Billy a full bath and added some of my sensual, relaxing bath beads to it. I lit several candles and placed them about the room. As I prepared Billy's exotic retreat, I thought of the reason I had picked this house above all the others that had been shown to us. I love the huge bathroom with the sunken tub and Jacuzzi. I smiled, as I put the finishing touches on my seductive plan. After putting on some soft, mellow music, I put on a sexy, lace teddy and lit some fragrant incense. I was ready for Billy. Upon entering the living room, I noticed that Billy had dozed off. While I was putting the blindfold on him, he slowly awakened with a lopsided grin on his face.

"What are you up to woman," he said curiously.

"I have a surprise for you sweetie," I uttered softly.

Grabbing him by the arms and pulling him to his feet, I led him slowly to the bathroom.

"Just trust me baby, you're in good hands."

After getting Billy to the bathroom, I began undressing him.

"You just stand right here and leave everything up to me, okay!"

"Now you really got me curious," he replied, "Whatever it is, I know that I'm enjoying it up to this point."

"Trust me baby, you're going to love the other things I have planned for you even more," I murmured, while unbuttoning his shirt, and trailing kisses on his neck and chest.

When I finished undressing him, I removed the blindfold.

"You like," I whispered seductively.

"I love it .... and I love you even more Lynnie," he spoke huskily.

Billy removed my lacy teddy and we slipped into the silky, scented water. I allowed him to sit between my legs, as I coaxed him into leaning back against me by wrapping my legs around his waist. Applying bath gelee to a sponge, I very lovingly bathed him all over, stopping to caress him occasionally. My sensual massage ignited fiery passions in him that made him moan in erotic pleasure. That massage did the trick. Billy turned around to face me, as he softly planted a shower pf miniature kisses down my neck. I was mesmerized by his sexy image. The soft glow that the candles cast over his glistening, muscular body was tantalizing.

"Now, it's your turn for a massage, baby," he said in a low sexy voice that made my heart race.

He spread bath gelee on the sponge and softly stroked my moist skin. I sat back this time between his legs, as he sensually cleansed my body. Billy's touch fully gratified my every nerve. I allowed myself to become totally indulged in the massage and the moment. He cupped each breast and gently sponged them until my nipples became hard peaks, swollen with anticipation. Billy had wet my appetite for more of his loving, as my body began responding to every delightful touch. Hr trailed soft kisses along my neck sending sharp, darts of desire through me. I met his lips in a kiss that was so deep and hungry that he knew my desire was raging. I could sense the change in his body immediately, as it matched a perfect tune with mine. Billy pulled his mouth away from mine abruptly.

"Oh God.... Lynnie.... you make me burn with desire like hell on fire," he whispered, his voice husky with unconcealed desire.

I had to smile at the look of so much passion in his eyes, as I admired his handsome features. He led me out of the tub, scooped me up in his strong arms, and carried me effortlessly to our bedroom.

We lay together side by side on the bed for several long seconds, as we were engulfed by each other's passion. Billy just stared at me for a moment as if he were taking in every little piece of me. His gaze traveled from my head to my bare breasts, pausing for a moment at the heart of my desire, as he softly rubbed my thigh.

"Woman .... you are so beautiful," he whispered.

He then covered my lips with his in a kiss that was so deep and filled with such longing that my veins felt as though fire were singeing them from the inside out. I sank my fingers into Billy's silky hair as he covered my breast with his seeking mouth. I gasped aloud as he licked circles around the first nipple, then the other until they were to pebble hardness. Another gasp of desire overtook me, as he began rubbing the tips of my breast teasingly between his fingers.

"The things that you do to me," he said huskily, while gazing into my eyes.

I gasped again, as he slid his hand down my stomach and buried his fingers lower. His swiftly indrawn breath and mild cursing excited me more than I could have imagined. The knowledge that I could elicit the same response from him that he got from me was intoxicating, like drinking heady wine.

Billy wrapped my legs around his waist and he gently eased into me, savoring my heat, feeling it, wanting it, and needing it. His want for me overwhelmed him when I lifted my hips to receive him. He gave up and gave in as the passion consumed him. I clung to Billy, as he held me tightly in his arms and whispered sweet love words. When we had reached the ultimate pitch, our bodies exploded in spasms of passionate waves of pleasure that touched each nerve in our bodies. Powerful shudders tore through us, as we reached our earth-shattering fulfillment simultaneously.

We lay together wrapped in each other's arms relishing our sweet lovemaking session.

"It was just what the doctor ordered," Billy said slowly, softly kissing me on my eyelid.

Thoughts about our supper suddenly popped in my mind. It had been forgotten after I got Billy up for his bath.

"Supper is probably cold by now," I murmured disappointedly.

"Yeah .... and I'm starving. Tell you what? Let's shower together and we can heat it up in the microwave, okay?" Billy suggested.

"Let's hit the shower. The last one in is a rotten egg!" I sang out.

So we raced for the shower.

* * * * * * *

After eating, we cuddled up on the sofa and watched T.V. Somehow, my mind drifted on my new friends that I had met at the park today.

"I met three of our neighbors today Billy. They are really nice people. Maybe we should ask them over for dinner one night," I said, seeking a response.

"Sure Lynnie, baby, that's fine," Billy remarked disillusioned.

"Billy -- did you really hear what I just said? I would like for you to meet them sometime Honey," I inquired again.

Baby--all you really need is me. Why do you need to have friends anyway? It has always been you and me.

Billy let out a big yawn, as he rose from the sofa.

"Lynnie, I think I'm going to turn in," he said wearily. "Are you coming?"

"In a little while, honey," I answered.

He kissed me goodnight and went to bed. I sat there wondering why he seemed so unconcerned about my new friends -- I just didn't understand. I watched T.V. for about ten minutes longer and decided to dismiss Billy's strange reaction, and go to bed.

THREE

Billy got promoted to Chief Engineer for his hard work and his concept of drafting. I was so proud of my husband and his accomplishments. Though, as proud as I was of Billy, and his achievements, his ambitions moved me and made me want to pursue my career. But I figured I would wait a little longer before I said anything.

The days lumbered by, and they turned into months, but I was patient and I occupied myself with making a quilt. My grandmother had insisted that I learn how to quilt some of the weekends that spent with her when I was growing up. I became rather good at it. After all these years, I found that it wasn't that hard to pick back up. I even sold a couple of them to a female colleague of Billy's who thought they were very beautiful and ornamental.

This particular day was just mediocre. It was very nice outside and the sun beamed in through the openings in the vertical blinds. I had been working on another quilt, sewing pieces together that would create the quilt top when I have enough of them sewn together.

I had been working on this quilt now for several hours and really needed a distraction. I could always pick the quilting back up anytime that I wanted. After all, quilting was just a hobby I had assumed .... a pastime to fill my day. Idle time never did do anything for me except make me restless. At an early age, my parents had instilled into me the importance of making constructive use of my idle time. Evidently this teaching has remained with me, even after reaching adulthood.

The ringing phone penetrated my thoughts.

"Hello Lynn.... How are you doing?' the voice chimed.

"Hi Sam.... Oh-h-h I'm fine.... How are you?" I asked back, trying to sound cheerful.

"I'm good. Hey.... What are you doing for lunch?"

"I was jus getting ready to raid the fridge. I had been working on a quilt, but I'd gotten bored and needed a break."

"Why don't you come over and eat with me and keep me company so that I won't have to eat alone?"

"Sure.... I'll be right over."

I went to the bathroom and freshened up and headed

over to Sam's place. The walk was very pleasant and getting out of the house was exactly what I needed.

The summer heat had yielded to a temporary cool front pushing through and, as always, I felt profound relief. I strolled down the sidewalk between rows of oaks and magnolias that were so big and old that they formed a canopy through which the sun shone through in dappled patches. The gray Spanish moss hanging from the trees stirred gently in the faint breeze.

Back a little ways from the narrow street were white houses with front and side porches. New sections on Lakeshore drive had brick houses, but on this old street the houses were all frame, all white, and all ample in size. I seemed to have a love-hate relationship with my new residence. I was never able to forget that many of the lovely old places now enshrined by preservationists had been built by black slaves, and that the wealth of the planters who'd established the town was made possible by slavery.

On the other hand, it was home and therefore a sustaining fabric of associations, events, and memories. Most of the time I was content here because of my husband, my newfound friends, and because I could get away when I needed to do so. I liked a suburban environment and found vitality in it. Charleston was much like Atlanta in that respect.

When I arrived at Sam's house, she greeted me at the door with a huge smile and a big hug.

"Come on in Lynn," Sam invited. "I hope that chicken salad and a fruit plate is good for you."

"Sounds great to me Sam. I feel like I'm starved.

"Go ahead and seat yourself Lynn. I need to get these rolls out of the oven. I already have us some ice tea fixed. I'll be right back"

I seated myself and admired the pretty setting of the table.

"You really do have a very lovely home Sam," I said admiring her ample kitchen.

"It's all right I guess," Sam remarked modestly, as she placed a basket of hot rolls and a dish of butter on the table.

"The salad looks great and the rolls smell heavenly," I said, spreading butter on a roll.

Sam and I chatted as we ate our salads. Sam was a history teacher at Ashley Hall High School. She was on her lunch break, but since she also had an extra hour of free time due to a study period, she often came home so that she could unwind and relax before her next class.

Sam and I chatted about various things as we consumed our salads, our fruit, and our rolls. We ended up talking about different shopping malls about South Carolina, which afterward, we concluded in making a date to go shopping and for her to expose me to some more of our fair city. I eagerly agreed to the shopping trip -- it sounded like fun.

Sam and I finished our lunch and I helped her wash

up the dishes and straighten up the kitchen.

Sam had to go back to school. Her lunchtime was over and she was due in class shortly.

"Girl, I have about fifteen minutes to get back to school. Want me to drop you off at home .... it's no problem.

"Oh no-o-o.... I want to walk back so that I can enjoy this beautiful day."

Okay.... Well I'll see you later, okay," Sam yelled, as she backed out of the driveway.

I waved back as she sped away. I stood and watched until she disappeared around the corner.

After returning home, I felt recharged. My lunch and visit with Sam seemed to rejuvenate me.

I strolled about the house, admiring everything about it. It was a very beautiful home that Billy and I shared.

My mind drifted back to when we were looking for the perfect home here. I knew just the type of home that I wanted for Billy and me. I think that I had kind of stressed the realtor out a little by my indecisiveness. I wasn't going to settle for anything less than the house I had laid out in my mind.

When I found this house, I remembered how my heels clattered through one of the empty rooms in particular, leaving an echo behind. It was a large, open room with an endless span of picture windows looking out on the Bay. The floor had beautiful, dark inlaid wood and there were bronze sconces on the walls.

I had told myself," *This is a remarkable view.*" I nodded pleasantly, but said nothing out loud. It was a beautiful view…. a splendid view. This was a very lovely house. Billy had said that he wanted a house.

When I stood in the dining room, it had the same view of the Bay. Turning around with my back to the window, there was a beautiful fireplace. It was a warm room with beam ceilings and bay windows instead of the flat picture window of the living room. I squinted and envisioned seeing white organdie curtains and plants, inviting cushions in the window seats, a soft white rug, and a rich, dark wood table…. I squinted again seeing it all, and began smiling to myself.

I remembered telling the realtor that I was going to take another look upstairs. The realtor nodded silently that time because she was tired. She had been doing this for three days, and there was nothing left to show. I had seen everything. Sunken living rooms, sweeping views, seven bedrooms, three bedrooms, wood paneling, marble floors, and crooked Victorians in need of work. I had seen everything from the decrepit to the divine in this suburban area. The realtor just sat down heavily in the window seat, and flipped through her book for the thirtieth time in three days. This was it I told myself. It was the last suitable home she had.

While I was upstairs, I looked out at the view from

the master bedroom. The Bay again, and the same cozy window seats that I had seen downstairs in the dining room, and the fireplace with the marble mantelpiece. There was an overwhelming friendliness to this place. I imagined Billy passing me in the hall and him pinching me on my behind as he reached into closet. I imagined having a son, and would be sitting in the window seat with him looking out over the Bay at twilight, talking about something important, like baseball or snakes. There were two other bedrooms on the second floor. One of the rooms was a large one, which faced the garden at the front of the house, with lots of sunshine and tall French windows. That room could be my son's room. And there was another room that was an equally pretty bedroom .... a guestroom perhaps. We probably didn't need one, but it was always good to have a spare room.

The kitchen I'd seen downstairs was open and warm, a room to have dinner in when Billy and I didn't have guests. It had two brick walls and a built-in barbeque, and the rest of it was painted blue with a blue ceramic floor. The tiles had been brought over from Portugal from the last tenants. It was perfect…. All it needed was copper pots, and a wrought-iron hook with salamis and peppers…. Glass jars filled with spices…. Curtains, and the butcher-block table Billy had in his kitchen right now. I was bringing very little from my place. Only a few treasured things, the pretty pieces I had acquired over the years. The ordinary, functional things Billy said that we could buy when we get a house.

I continued on my mental journey, looking around the room that could be my future son's room again, and down at the well-tended little garden. High hedges that would give privacy surrounded it. In fact, the house seemed to be equipped with everything we needed. The view and the fireplaces and high ceilings Billy had said was a must, an elegant sweeping staircase that led upstairs, and three bedrooms, which even gave them a spare. Everything that this house had to offer was just what the two of us wanted. I sat on the top of the stair and looked up. Directly over my head was a skylight, and to my right was a slightly open door. More closets maybe? I leaned backward to take a look. It looked like a stairway. I frowned and got up, calling down to the realtor still waiting downstairs.

"Is there more upstairs?" I called out to her.

There was the sound of shuffling through the now familiar book, and then a vague *"I'm not sure."* And then as I walked toward the door, the realtor came to the foot of the stairs. *"Maybe some kind of attic. But it doesn't say anything about it in the book. It just says here three bedrooms, den, and maids'."*

"Den?" I hadn't seen a den. There was a den I thought.

The stairway was narrow but carpeted, and the walls had new-looking beige silk tapestry. It hardly looked like the kind of thing you'd put on the way to the attic. As I reached the top of the stairs, I saw why. This was no attic, and it wasn't even a den. It was a small, well-proportioned room with wood-paneled walls, a fireplace, and a 360-degree view of the Bay and the hills leading south. The room was well carpeted, boasted the now familiar bay windows, and there was even a little extension to it, a kind of solarium, which would be heavenly filled with plants. Also, this would make me a great office if I decided to pursue writing or wanted a home office. There would be plenty of room for a desk and file cabinets. The extension had two discreet, glass French doors, which did not impair the view, but still allowed one to shut oneself off…. it was the perfect office. For Billy and me, it could also be a special hideaway, a room to fill with beauty and children and love. The whole house was that way. It was exactly what we wanted. Better than that…. It was exactly what I'd dreamed of, but thought I would never find. This house possessed beauty, elegance, simplicity, warmth, privacy, and convenience.

"We'll take it." I said in a decisive voice as I turned to the realtor, who had now followed me upstairs.

"It's a remarkable place," the woman agreed.

I nodded victoriously. *"It's perfect."* I was beaming. I could hardly wait to show Billy. *"How soon can we have it?"*

"Tomorrow." The realtor grinned. They had done it after all. She couldn't get over this. She had been sure

this sale would be a hopeless one. This woman wanted everything and wouldn't settle for less. But the upstairs room did make this house and incredible find. Why the hell hadn't someone else grabbed it up? Maybe no one else had noticed the upstairs room before. It sure wasn't on the listing. *"It says here that it's available immediately. We can draw up the contract and it's yours."*

"I really ought to show it to -- my fiancé. But I'm absolutely sure. This is it. In fact, just to be sure of it -- how much do they require as a down payment?" The realtor checked her book again and came up with a most unexceptionable figure. I wanted to shriek, *"That's all?"*, but I kept quiet. This one was too good to blow. I hastily wrote out a check and handed it to the woman. *"I'll bring my fiancé back tonight."*

I did too, and he fell in love with it as I had.

"Isn't it great?" I said excitedly.

With Billy I could be indulgent.

"Oh Billy, I love it!" I said, as I plunked down in one of the window seats with a huge smile.

"I love the house -- and I love you." He walked over to me with a peaceful smile, and then looked out at the Bay. *"It's going to look terrific with you and possibly a few kids running around in it."*

"Do you think we should take it?"

I was smiling at him like a child, anxious and excited and proud.

Billy laughed. *"You're asking me? I thought that it was already settled, sweetheart. I owe you for that down payment, by the way. I expect to support you fully. You deserve it and I love you Lynnie.*

Billy sat down on the window seat beside me. *"I promise to always love you and provide for you."*

A backfiring car snapped me back to the present. I realized that I had to get supper ready for Billy. I prepared the meal in record time and none too soon. Just as I finished setting the table, Billy breezed in.

"Hi sweetheart…. I'm totally wiped out. Today was rough and intense."

Billy walked up and kissed me lightly on the cheek.

"I'm pretty beat to honey from working in the house."

Billy and I ate our meal and had a light conversation about our day. When we finished eating, Billy went upstairs to take a shower while I cleaned up the kitchen and washed up our dishes.

When I made it upstairs, Billy had already gotten into bed. I took a shower and soon joined my husband in bed. I got in bed and snuggled up to him and he put his arms around me and pulled me close. I felt so happy and secure and loved. This comforting feeling soon was replaced by contented sleep, as I lay tucked away safely in my husband's arms.

Chapter

FOUR

It was a fantastic June morning as my eyes slowly opened to the new day. I climbed out of bed, went to the bathroom and washed up, and headed downstairs to begin breakfast. Billy soon followed after taking his shower and shave.

While Billy and I ate our breakfast, he surprised me with his next statement. "Lynn honey…. You know…. we haven't been back home since we moved here to Charleston nearly six months ago. How about we go home for a visit this weekend? Do you want to?"

Sitting there gawking at Billy with my jaw dropped, I finally stammered out the words, "Uh…. Uh…. Okay. That would be great. I'd love to see my family."

"We can leave early Saturday morning. It is seven-hour drive, so we should get top Atlanta by noon if we leave at five o'clock in the morning. So why don't you get us some things packed today, okay?"

"Got to get to work," Billy said, rising from his chair. He walked over to me and kissed me good-bye. Then turning quickly on his heel, disappeared out the door.

After Billy had gone to work, I cleaned up the breakfast dishes. I poured another cup of coffee and sat back down at the kitchen table. As I slowly sipped the coffee, my mind drifted to thoughts of getting a chance to go back home for a visit. My mind entered a portal in time back when I was a small girl…. back when my family and I lived in a rural district of Atlanta. I'd had a great childhood growing up and my mother and father loved my older sister, my younger brother, and I very much and raised us all up in hopes of us becoming responsible, well-balanced adults.

Remembering back when I was younger, I was second oldest of three siblings…. and there was my older sister Catherine and my younger brother Willie. Back then, we didn't think that much about some of the things we did. Now that we all have grown up, we marvel at the way our father and mother handled us.

For one thing, our father made work fun. We didn't make a fuss about things that we had to do and I would venture to say that we all worked hard, but our mother and father always worked right along with us. They would never ask us to do nothing that they would not do themselves.

During the winter months when we needed wood for the furnace, our father would hitch horses to a sled or wagon, depending on the weather, and we were off to get some wood. I don't know how or when our father did it, but somehow during the week he found the time to go back and cut the wood to be brought to the house. If it had snowed, he would allow us to hook our little sleds onto the back of the bobsled.

I our father saw that we were getting tired of carrying and loading the wood on the sled, he would keep reminding us of how nice and warm it was going to make the house. This inspired us to carry more wood. When we returned home, our mother always had hot cocoa waiting for us before we had to go and unload the wood and place it in the cellar. Mother always had cocoa for us kids, even when we had been doing anything that was cold.

Mother, at least a couple of times a week, would have hot bread waiting for us when we got home from school. You would have thought that it would have discouraged her when we devoured a whole loaf on the spot when we got into the house. We always had all the milk, eggs, butter, apples, potatoes and basic foods that we wanted and never once got to know anything about being hungry. We were blessed with food.

When we got older, we had curfews -- regardless of

age. At the time, we thought our father was being very strict with us, but later in life we saw that it was done for our protection. As long as we lived under their roof, we had to obey their rules. Daddy figured that twelve o'clock p.m. was late enough for anyone to be out and said that there was nothing going on that was worthwhile after that time. We thought that he was cruel when we all had friends that didn't have to keep such strict hours. However, that was just the way it was.

After we had grown up, it seemed so strange to us kids to go somewhere for a dinner and the Mothers would see that their little ones had their meals first. When we had family get-togethers, like Christmas, Thanksgiving, the parents and older folks always sat at the first table to eat while the kids just played with our cousins etc, until the first table was finished with their meal. They never hurried and often sat around the table visiting. Then our Mother would clear the tables for the kids to eat.

We had such a good sliding hill in the winter. Neighbor kids liked to come to slide down hill with us. This hill was across Rt. 58 on Mrs. West's place. At that time it was no problem to cross Rt. 58 either. This hill was the closest thing to a mountain we could ever imagine. Today every one of us kids look over there and wonder where that big hill went to - it seemed so big to us. It had a little mound of dirt at the bottom and either you could go over that (we called it the shoot-the-shoot), or you could turn your sled to go around a corner toward the creek, usually getting wet.

I wonder how Mother ever kept us in dry clothes, as we did not even know dryers existed. She made all our mittens - with three kids, which were quite a few mittens. It seemed so far from the house to that hill and you usually would just get over there and would have to go to the bathroom so rather than trudging all the way home, you just wet your pants and let them freeze. You never seemed to mind if the sliding was really fun, but if not so good then the wet pants seemed much worse. Again, as soon as we would get back home, Mother would usually have hot cocoa for us to drink while getting warm. There wasn't anything like Mother's fresh, warm tapioca pudding. We never seemed to even let it get completely cooled. Even to this day, I cannot make tapioca pudding without leaving nearly a dishful in the pan to eat while really warm.

When I was quite small, I discovered Daddy had about the neatest initials in the whole world - spelling MAT. I got hold of a paintbrush and some paint and painted his initials as big as I could on the foundation of the house. I thought I was doing such a good job of marking Daddy's possessions with his initials, but Daddy did not think the same. He got a can of gasoline and a scrub brush and made me clean all those initials off. It was not latex paint either and did not come off very well.

Daddy was so soft hearted. He had an Uncle Cy that lived in Michigan. After a war, possibly the Civil War, this Uncle Cy was in a prison. When the song came out "Cool, Cool Water", Daddy could not stand to listen to it without having big tears in his eyes. He would tell us that Uncle Cy told him about being in this prison and they would not even be given water to drink. They would get so thirsty they would lick the foundation walls for the moisture on them. This would just get to Daddy whenever he would hear that song.

A lot of the things we remember about living with the folks were in later years, but when we were all little and Mother and Daddy were young, they used to do so many things with us.

We usually, once a year, would have a Church picnic down to Elyria at Cascade Park. The men would usually get a ballgame going, but Mother was always fun and did things with us kids. They had a great big slide - it must have been nearly a mile long, but they have since shortened it. One time Mother went down that big slide, she was probably holding onto Catherine, but somehow her arm went along the wooden edge and burned her arm so badly. It must have hurt so terribly but she did not complain.

In the fall, Daddy would somehow find a day and it would be apple-picking time. Then, when we got home from school, we had to go pick up the ones that had fallen, the ones from trees that only had cider apples so that Daddy could take them to the cider mill to make the cider. Those nights would usually be cold, rainy, wet -sometimes snow…. a very cold job. Daddy again was always telling us how good that cider was going to taste.

When studying in the evening we would have either cider and popcorn or apples and popcorn. We all still seem to love those things -- popcorn, cider and apples.

Often on Sunday afternoon Mother would make us candy. She could make the best fudge but later Catherine learned to make peanut butter fudge and Mother thought it was better than hers so Catherine usually made the peanut butter fudge.

There was a time that Daddy had gotten Mother a new carpet for the living room. We were all so proud of that carpet and then that was when they moved Grandpa George in to live with us. Grandpa would smoke and spit, always sitting right in front of the little gas heater. Daddy finally had to put stuff down to try to protect Mother's new carpet but Grandpa still often missed his bucket. He burned several holes in that new carpet also. Sometimes it almost seemed like he did things on purpose but he probably didn't.

Daddy had a pet name for Mother - "Sal" or "Sally". It was not long before Grandpa would start calling Mother this when he wanted her to do something for him and he would call - "Sally". This used to make us so irritated with him - that was Daddy's pet name for Mother and not Grandpa's and we did not like it.

Catherine and I did not really get along with Grandpa very well - I guess we were too young. He always seemed annoyed with us, never knew our names. Our brother Willie did not seem to have the same feelings about Grandpa as Catherine and I did.

At this time, Catherine and I were both taking music lessons and Grandpa did not like to hear us practice. He would yell at Mother to have us stop. Mother would then tell us to go out to the shed to practice. Catherine and I never wanted to practice so much as when we knew it annoyed him. Sometimes Mother would complain to Daddy about Grandpa yelling at us but Daddy never argued with Grandpa.

I feel bad that I do not have nice memories of Grandpa George like the older ones do, or like the McConnell cousins have, but he was never very nice to either Catherine or me. Now Grandma Whitney was something else, she was so laid back, fun, gentle and kind - we just loved her.

Somehow even though money was not very plentiful, Mother gave us piano lessons. Ida was the first and she was a very good pianist and played at Church for many, many years.

I had my first lessons with Olive McConnell and she was fun. Then Mother hired Floyd Moore to come to the house to give me lessons. He was some shirttail relation, having married Aunt Geneva's sister. I always thought he was a little strange. I know I did not practice very well for him and he always knew it. He was such a sissy guy - nothing like Daddy.

When we were quite young and before Ida had started playing the piano very much, nearly every Sunday night we would go into the parlor and Mother would play the piano so we all could sing. Mother was a very good player and Daddy a good singer. When Mother played the hymn, "His Eye is on the Sparrow" she would always start to cry and told us that had been Grandpa Whitney's favorite hymn.

We had some really funny times at the table after Grandpa came to live us. We had strict rules before, but nothing like then. Grandpa always had to say the grace before eating and the more we wanted to eat, the longer he would make his Grace prayers. If you complained, he would just make them that much longer. We rather resented that he wanted to sit at the head of the table as Daddy had always sat there, but Daddy said it was easier for Grandpa to sit there, as he wasn't crowded.

Grandpa would try to eat peas, of all things, with his knife and us kids would all get to snicker. Mother would have such a hard time to try to get us to stop. When there are three kids and one starts giggling, it is hard not for the others to do the same.

Then Grandpa would pour his coffee into his saucer to cool and drink from the saucer. He had long whiskers and would slurp his coffee through the whiskers so that would about crack us up. He would then glare at us over the top of his glasses, and then this would send us into the giggles again. We could not leave the table without being excused - that was a rule long before Grandpa came, but sometimes Mother would excuse us a bit faster if she see things were just hanging on to keep us there. She knew…

One of the things I remember is that we always ate meals together. Breakfast was usually oatmeal as Mother insisted we have something hot in our tummies before going to school - warm weather or cold.

Mother and Daddy went to Church pretty often, but when Catherine and I were very little they did not always go but they would send the older ones. I remember one time Willie had acted up in Church and Uncle Ed and Aunt Lois stopped on the way home to tell Mother and Daddy about that and he got punished. When we all went to church, since we sat on straight chairs, we would take up a whole row with the three of us kids and Mother and Daddy. When the Catherine got bigger, she liked to sit with her friends, and then we did not need the whole row.

We could never understand, but on special occasions like Christmas and Easter, there would be so many other people that would come to Church and everyone would be making such a fuss over them, but we had to go every Sunday and nobody made a fuss over us - something did not seem right.

We could never wait until Easter to see what kind of a hat Mrs. Beard would be wearing. Her son Jack was very artistic and loved to make hats for her. They were always just so pretty but so different.

Now that so many houses have air conditioning, which we think we cannot live without, we wonder did we used to have such warm weather years ago, but we did.

Some nights it seemed like that upstairs was so hot you could not get to sleep. We would call back and forth to each other's rooms if we thought they might have a cool breeze coming in their window. If one thought it was cooler in their room, we would then haul our mattress off a bed; draw it down that hall to the room with a breeze. About then the breeze would come from another way or else Daddy would call up the stairs and tell us to settle down and get to sleep. In the winter it was just as cold in some of the rooms, or rather in all the rooms. There were radiators in every room but often would not work. It was so great to come home from school to find out Daddy had been working on the radiator in your room and you once again had heat.

We always had so much pride in the home place and we all worked so hard to make it the nice place that it was. When we were very little we would always mow the lawn when many people just turned animals in their yards to keep the grass down. Catherine and I were so little we could not mow the lawn by ourselves but would tie a rope onto the front of the mower and one would pull while the other one pushed, but we still kept our lawn mowed so pretty.

We had a long front walk that went from the front porch to the road, then steps down the bank to the road. We would trim that and keep the grass from growing over the walkway. Mother always had lots of pretty flowers so the yard was truly a pretty place. Mother planted a snowball bush beside the walk which when it got big was really too close to the walk. On a wet, rainy morning there was just no way of getting past that bush without getting drenched. Mother had been at Daddy to cut it back and trim it up and he had probably heard this about long enough so he trimmed it alright -he cut it back to the roots. Mother *was* sure he had killed it, but the next year it came back but for some reason he did keep it trimmed better after that.

We also had an old yucca plant in the front yard and when wrestling with each other, the ultimate goal was to throw the other one into the yucca plant. That stopped the wrestling I assure you -- that thing was wicked.

Mother had lots of patience with us but she could never stand us arguing -- especially at the table. Sometimes when Mother was not nearby we could get going but you soon learned you did not want to argue if Mother was close enough to hear you.

Sundays were meant for a day of rest. Daddy did his chores but no more than absolutely necessary.

We would then go to church, have dinner and then usually Daddy wanted a nap. Sometimes, or really quite often, after he had a nap, he would get up and then *we* would all go for a ride.

The first car I really remember was a big old Buick touring car with side curtains. It had two little seats in the back, which let down, called jump seats. These were usually for Catherine and me.

On a nice Sunday afternoon, with the side curtains up, with Willie always having the outside seat so he could get the entire breeze and away we would go. Our favorite place to go was down by Huntington to what I suppose is New London-Eastern Road as that had lots of little hills and curves on it. Daddy would put his cap on backwards and tell us he was Fred Oldsfield and away we would go so fast down that road, we would be hollering and laughing on every hill. Mother would keep telling Daddy to be careful but we thought we were really a wild bunch. I think that was the car that had a cutout on it and when we would be going the fastest, Daddy would pull this cut out which made a lot of noise.

It seemed like nearly everyone at our school was related. When I was going, there were Billie and Paul Bradley, Don and Mary J. Whitlock, Gregory Westbrook, Carl, Francis, Kim, Eleanor Beasley, Aaron Finney, Ethel Waite, Barry Sims, Pam, Valerie and Walter Green, Floyd

Calvin and Mary E. Whitney, Ida, Dorothy, Willie, Catherine and myself.

My first teacher was Evelyn Marshal, then Ella Hicks, Emma Bradford-Sheffield then Aunt Eva. It was hard for Aunt Eva as she was related to nearly all of us. She was such a favorite Aunt but she could be strict in school but she did not want to show any partiality so she had to be a bit hard on us.

At noontime, especially in the winter, we would hurry through our lunches, or else take our lunch with us and hurry over to John West's pond to ice skate. Gregory Westbrook was such a good skater and had regular skates, but he always took the time to help us to skate and to help us clamp on our old skates. It was just so hard to hear the teacher's bell from over on that pond so many times we just did not hear it and were very late getting back. The teacher never said much.

We played lots of ball while going to school. Gregory again was a good ball player and I must have been through the grade school before I realized girls didn't always have four chances to bat at home plate. I could not catch the ball very good either and when out in the field, would just stand there and pray that the dumb ball would not come my way. Still I always enjoyed playing ball.

Skating, whether at school or at home, was one of my favorite things to do in the winter. Daddy would chop holes in the pond for the cows to drink but sometimes would also clean off the pond for skating. I would get back there as soon as I could after coming home from school and sometimes would not even hear Mother when she called for supper.

A ringing doorbell snapped me back from my reverie.

When I answered the door, a Jehovah Witness representative was standing there smiling broadly holding a stack of booklets. We spoke briefly and then she offered me several of her booklets. I accepted the booklets and thanked the lady for them.

Walking back to the living room, I decided to call my mother and let her know that Billy and I were coming home to visit and that they could expect us by tomorrow afternoon. My mother was ecstatic and said that she would let the rest of the family know and get them all over to the house.

After hanging up the phone, I smiled to myself. I knew that my mother was going to cook up all sorts of food. It would be a full-fledged cookout.

I did a few chores around the house and then started preparation for supper. I wanted Billy to have a special meal tonight because it was wonderful of him to suggest that we go home for a visit. I decided on smoked salmon.

After starting supper, I went upstairs to get our things packed for our trip tomorrow. I was so looking forward to going home. I hadn't realized just how much I had missed my family and the Atlanta's own unique characteristics.

With the packing done, I went downstairs to check on supper. The salmon was coming along very nicely. So I put on some sweet peas with pearl onions and made a strawberry cheesecake for dessert.

It was five o'clock and Billy will be home very soon. Supper was just about ready. I only needed to put the finishing touches on it. As I began setting the table, Billy strolled in.

Billy and I sat down and ate together. He discussed how his day was and I told him about mine. I always enjoyed this time with Billy. This was our time to reconnect after a long day.

After supper, Billy and I prepped for bed because we had an early day tomorrow. As we climbed into bed together, Billy pulled me into his arms, kissed me gently on the forehead, and said goodnight.

Chapter

FIVE

Bright and early the next morning Billy and I were off to Atlanta. The drive back home was scenic and it was a beautiful day and we both were enjoying the sights along the way. I had picked up some brochures about some of the tourist attractions that were between Charleston and Atlanta. Even though we wouldn't have time to really indulge in the sights, we could observe them momentarily.

Just over the Georgia border and approximately a two-hour drive from Charleston lays the charming city of Savannah. Savannah was a visual delight with its stately mansions, moss-draped oaks, and massive churches. I had read in the brochure that Savannah is also known as one of the best walking cities and that walking was the best way to really appreciate Savannah's historic squares, azalea-laden parks, and eighteenth century cemeteries. Savannah has lots of antique shops and art galleries and there is a festive assortment of music, food, and activities that always seem to be taking place.

About three and half hours from Charleston, Billy and I came to the delightful city of Greenville, which is nestled in the foothills of the Appalachians Mountains. The brochure said that downtown Greenville offered 64 restaurants -- many with alfresco dining. Students from the Governor's School for the Performing Arts often serenade diners with street performances of classical music. Broadway touring companies and renowned musical artists perform year-round at the Peace Center in downtown Greenville.

Just a short drive from Greenville is Table Rock State Park. It is the location of an enormous boulder that leaves hikers and other visitors equally breathless. According to legend, the boulder served as the dining table of a giant chieftain.

After a few more hours of driving, Billy and I arrived at my Mom and Dad's home. Everyone came out to greet us -- Mom, Dad, Catherine, Willie, Aunt Geneva, Uncle Cy, Grandpa George, Grandma Whitney, and a horde of cousins, nieces, and nephews.

Grandma Whitney looked hard at me when I walked up.

"Well…. It's about time you were coming home to see us," she said, as she threw her arms around me and kissed me on the cheek. "You need some real down-home cooking…. you're looking kind of peaked and thin."

"What did you and Grandma Whitney cook? Everything smells so good," I asked.

The grill had smoke pouring out of the chimney and the aroma of the meat mixed with the hickory chips and charcoal was delightful.

Grandma Whitney served the meal. There were savory chicken with tender dumplings, minted carrots, green beans, turnip greens, a dish of sliced red tomatoes, ribs, and hot links. The food was scrumptious and it was great to see my family -- it was really good to be home.

* * * * * * * *

There was a party in works for Grandma Whitney's birthday tomorrow. After eating, Billy went to see his parents and several of my cousins and me went shopping.

My cousins and I all climbed into the car and away we went, whizzing down Lincoln Boulevard.

"Which mall," Kim asked, as she turned into LaSalle Street.

"Fairview," Valerie said.

We hit one store after another, trying on different outfits and shoes. I had almost forgotten how much I used to enjoy shopping this mall.

"What else is on your list?" Pam asked me an hour later.

"One more belt, black leather, and it has to be two inches wide," I said.

"We still don't have Grandma Whitney's gift," Kim sad, shifting three shopping bags to one arm s tat se could put her other one through mine.

"Valerie, did you have something in mind for Grandma Whitney?" I asked.

"Not really. Any suggestions?"

"I got hr three piece sage suit. Would you like to buy her some jewelry to wear with it?" I asked suggestively.

In another fifteen minutes the belt was found and a pair of earrings that were hand-painted in rose and sage.

"See…. they're a perfect match for the suit," I said, smiling triumphantly of my idea.

"Let's get some coffee before we return home," Valerie suggested.

"Hey, that sounds good. There's a coffee shop right around the corner," Kim said.

When we arrived home, we brought our bags into the kitchen. I put on a pot of gourmet vanilla coffee, while Kim, Valerie, and Pam got out the wrapping paper and prepped our purchase for wrapping.

After the coffee was made, we drank coffee and got all of Grandma Whitney' gifts wrapped for tomorrow. Kim and Valerie brought me up to speed on the happenings in our hometown since I'd left.

After a few hours my cousins went home to work on their part of tomorrow's dinner. I poured half a cup of coffee and sat down at the kitchen table. As I sat there indulging in the aroma and flavor of the vanilla coffee, Mama entered the kitchen. She walked up to me and kissed me lovingly on the forehead as only a mother can do.

"I'm so happy that you are home Lynn. I hope that you and Billy are happy together and stay that way."

"I am happy Mama…. and Billy and I will stay happy…. always."

"That's good sweetheart…. As long as you are happy, I'm happy," Mama replied, placing her hand gently on my cheek.

"Well my dearest…. I'm going to bed now. I love you," Mama said, as she left the room.

I heard the front door close. Shortly afterward, Billy walked in.

"Hi Billy…. how are you parents?" I asked concerned.

"They're fine…. just arguing ad fighting as usual."

"Did you find everything that you were looking for when you went to the mall today?"

"Yes…. everything turned out great. Grandma Whitney will have a lot of nice gifts for tomorrow."

"Sure smells good in here. That ham smells great."

"It still needs to cook a while longer so I will be up for a while."

"Okay honey… I'm beat and I think I'll all it a night."

"Sleep tight sweetie," I said, smiling openly.

Billy kissed me lightly on the lips and disappeared out the door.

I got up from the table and checked on the rest of my part of tomorrow's dinner. I was making candied yams and a three-bean salad. The yams were done, so I peeled them and prepared them for then oven, alternating thick slices with orange and pineapple slices. I put butter, brown sugar, and spices over all, and then the large baking dish went into the oven.

I removed the ham, basted it, and returned it back to the oven.

After about another hour, I removed the ham and the yams from the oven. I made room in the fridge for the both, placed them inside, and decided to call it a night. Tomorrow would be Grandma's birthday and I wanted to be rested for it.

* * * * * * *

I arose early and got started working on Grandma Whitney's birthday dinner. Shortly after beginning my work in the kitchen, Kim, Valerie, and Pam arrived with their parts of the dinner. We all teamed up and prepared the rest of the dinner menu for today's festivities. We wanted to have everything ready by noon.

I filled a stockpot half full of water and put it on to get hot.

"Tell me what I can do to help," Kim said, as she watching me put a generous amount of seasoning in the pot.

"We want to help too," Pam and Valerie chimed in.

"Okay…. Kim you can shuck the corn and break the ears in half while I finish scrubbing the potatoes. We're not going to clean the shrimp. They will go in whole after they're washed, but with the shells on because it all helps add more flavor to the stew, okay?"

"Valerie…. You and Pam can cut some of the smoked ham and sausage into one-inch pieces."

Kim brought over a little pile of corn.

"Now what?"

"We put the potatoes in the pot to cook for about twenty minutes, and then we'll add the sausage.

Everything seemed to be in readiness. I lifted the heavy pot from the stove to the counter where the long serving platter waited to receive the succulent food. With tongs in hand, I lifted the stew from its broth.

It was eleven thirty and we were putting the finishing touches on dinner. Pam, Valerie, Kim, and I had been working diligently to make Grandma Whitney's birthday dinner a success.

"What a feast!" Kim exclaimed when she saw the platter with its pile of steaming shrimp in the center surrounded by small new potatoes, the corn, and the sausage.

"Grandpa George didn't like his stew this way. In fact, he used to add crab to his stew. Remember?" I reminded of a time back when we were much younger.

Stories surrounding the stew brought on other stories of Low country life, and the room brimmed with frequent laughter.

We all lingered at the table a long time reminiscing about childhood events.

After setting the table, we put together the three-bean salad. By the looks of it, everything was all set for the dinner.

Daddy pulled up in front of the house with Grandma and Grandpa, along with Catherine and her husband Frank and Willie and his wife Linda.

"Right on time," I said, looking at my watch and with much satisfaction in my achievement.

Both cars emptied and everyone came inside. Kim, Valerie, and Pam all greeted Grandma, and I too walked up to greet her and kissed her on the cheek.

"Happy birthday Grandma," I said admirably.

These old eyes of much wisdom studied me, glowing and stylist in a shawl collar maroon suit with matching earrings and hat. She patted me on my cheek fondly.

"Dinner is ready Grandma.... come on into the

kitchen," I said, taking her back the hand.

Billy pulled out her chair at the head of the table and seated her and then we all took our seats too.

Daddy said grace. Lifting his glass of sparkling grape juice, he proposed a toast:

'To my mother, with loving thanks for her blessed good life and the all the love and care for all of us here at this table today. May God continue to bless her and bless all of us to have many more happy years with her."

After Daddy's toast, Grandma only had this to say, "It would be hard to have a family that is better than the one I have. I love all of you."

We all joined hands, one to another, all the way around the table, as we all lovingly admired Grandma. All of us had so much love for this very wise lady.

The table really was a vision to behold. On the table was a succulent brown roast surrounded by over-browned potatoes, a large bowl of mixed green (turnips, mustard, and kale), with short cuts of bacon, a baking dish of candied yams, and the juicy ham all decorated with whole cloves, cherries, and pineapple slices, three-bean salad, bread and butter pickles, a platter of tomato slices alternated with Bermuda onion slices drizzled with oil, vinegar, and honey, two large baskets of hot rolls, one at each end of the table, homemade lemon pound cake and vanilla ice cream. Practically all of food on this menu was Grandma's favorite foods.

After eating, Grandma opened all of her gifts. My gift of the three-piece suit seemed to gain admiration from everyone. Grandma absolutely adored it.

I sat down beside Grandma and looked fondly into her eyes.

"I love you Grandma."

"I love you too baby…. And I love my suit," she said hugging me.

"You know Grandma…. Billy and I got to go. I wish that we could stay longer, but the miles between here and Charleston aren't going to get any closer."

"I know sweetheart…. You and Billy have a safe trip back home now you here? You come back and see your old grandma again," Grandma said, holding my face between both of her hands and kissing me.

"I've got some ham and other stuff fixed up for you and Billy to with you Lynn," Kim said, placing her hand on my shoulder.

Billy and I said our good-byes and we headed back for Charleston. I dozed on and off along the way. Before too long, we were pulling into our driveway.

Billy and I got ready for bed. The weekend had gone by so quickly, but I thoroughly enjoyed every minute of it. I hadn't realized just how tired I was until I lay down. The bed felt so good.

As I curled up next to Billy, I was so happy and content with life. The trip back home to see my family was just what I needed.

"Thank you Billy for the visit back home."

"Sure honey…. that was no problem. I'm glad that it made you happy."

"It did make me happy…. and I love you for doing that for me."

"I love you Lynnie."

Billy kissed me on the forehead and pulled me into his arms. Very shortly thereafter, things were was quiet and I fell into a dreamless, peaceful sleep.

Chapter
SIX

As I my eyes opened this Saturday morning, the sun had been up long before I had. Sunlight glistened through the bedroom as if it were late in the day. I glanced at the clock, which displayed eight o'clock. I usually don't sleep in that late, but this morning was different. I was going to be alone this weekend. Billy had to be away the entire weekend for a business trip to Los Angeles. I felt like I didn't have a reason to get up early since he was gone. I had no one to cook for, as I had grown accustomed. I was just plain lonely and missed him terribly. Even knowing that this was part of his job offered me little solace and made his absence no less bearable.

Instead of lying in bed and feeling sorry for myself, I forced myself to get up. I got up and washed my face and brushed my teeth. I changed into a pair of jeans and a white button-down cotton shirt. I pulled my hair back into a ponytail and put on a pair of sneakers and went to make some coffee.

I started the coffee and grabbed a bagel and some cream cheese, fixed a bowl of cereal and milk, and poured a glass of orange juice. At least this would be a breakfast that I would not to cook.

After finishing of my cereal, bagel and juice, I poured myself a cup of coffee and went out to the patio. As I sat sipping on the hot coffee and trying to figure out what I would do with myself, the phone rang.

"What's up girlfriend? How are you?" the voice rang out.

"I'm okay Sam…. Just a bit lonely since Billy's away on his business trip."

"I know just the thing to cure that loneliness…. Let's go shopping."

Suddenly, my spirits were uplifted and a smile eased over my face. I loved shopping.

"Sure Sam…. I'd love too."

"Well…. Dee and I will swing by and pick you up shortly and we'll be off, okay?"

"Okay…. I'll be ready."

After hanging up the phone, I rushed upstairs to my room and retrieved my purse and checked my hair in the bathroom mirror. I released my hair from the ponytail and quickly grabbed a comb and combed through it. I applied a little make-up and then hurried downstairs.

As I reached the bottom of the stairs, the doorbell rang.

When I opened the door, Sam stood there smiling solemnly.

"Are you ready girl?"

"Yes I am…. Let's go."

When we arrived at the mall, I was ready for the excitement. I really enjoyed going to the mall. I like the thrill of shopping and the crowds. Some people seem to get upset whenever they are in crowds. I personally think that the crowds give the season more meaning. I like to sit in the food court to rest and eat pretzels and watch all the people. It's interesting to me to see how different people act, dress and shop. Interestingly, I get my second wind and I'm good to go again.

Once we were parked, we all headed inside. We were at Mt. Pleasant Towne Centre and it was filled with many stores and boutiques.

Our first stop was Casual Corner Annex. They had plenty of beautiful and stylist outfits. I think that each of us chose a couple of hot outfits. The next stop was Victoria's Secret. There was so much pretty and sexy lingerie in here. We each tried on stuff…. all sorts of lacy, silky pieces. Our next stop was Liz Claiborne Shoes where they had shoes galore…. so many pretty and sexy styles.

After all of this shopping, we needed to replenish ourselves. We chose to go to the Longhorn Steakhouse and ordered the steak special with the baked potato and sour cream and we topped it off with homemade bread pudding with bourbon sauce. We people watched as we sat and enjoyed our meals and we chatted about our purchases.

After such a big meal, it was time for more shopping. We went to Chico's, Bed Bath and Beyond, Belk of Mt. Pleasant, and Old Navy. We had a ball trying on different outfits and modeling for each other.

After all of this shopping, it was getting late so we decided that we had done enough damage for one day. We left the mall and headed for home.

The late afternoon drive home was very nice. A moderate scented breeze flowed through the sunroof, as we whizzed down the street. We were all hyped up from our shopping spree and looked forward to sporting our new outfits.

When we arrived at my house, I got out and removed my bags. Sam and Dee waved good-bye as I watched them round the corner. I went inside and carried my bags to the bedroom. After sitting the bags on the floor, I plopped down on the side of the bed and fell spread-eagle across it. I was a bit tired from all of the shopping, yet content with myself. I had fun with Sam and Dee today and it was just the medicine I needed to cure the lonely blues that was consuming me. I thought about how nice it was to have some friends to just hang out with now and again. Whenever Billy was at work or away on business, having friends that I could do things with sometimes helped the loneliness and the void left by his absence. It is true that we had a very beautiful home, but I couldn't interact physically or emotionally with it. Billy seemed intent in believing that all I needed was him. He didn't want me to work and he preferred that I had no friends. I had a lot of trouble understanding the latter part of his preference -- the part about not having friends. Now that was a strange notion. What harm was there I thought in having a few friends? I just was not able to grasp that concept and his way of reasoning about this subject. He very tactfully avoids elaborating on the subject of Sam and Dee and he's never really very cordial to them whenever he's around them. I felt s though I was caught between a rock and a hard place. On one hand, I wanted to please my husband and respect his wishes. But on the other hand, I wanted to have friends that I could occasionally hang out with and do things with. I really didn't have a clue as to how to solve this dilemma.

Since I loved and enjoyed long, soaking, hot baths so much, I opted to draw a fragrant bath. These baths served as a means of relaxation as well as an escape whenever I was troubled and had something on my mind. I drew my bath and added one of my favorite scented oils and placed several candles about the room. Pulling my hair up into a high ponytail, I shed my clothing and slipped into the warm, soft, scented water. I positioned the bath pillow behind my head and lay back against it. The aroma of my bath and the warm water stared to relax away all my cares, as I succumbed to the delightful feeling. Lying there in the bath, I watched the candlelights gently flicker and sway. My relaxing, scented sanctuary lulled me into a light, dreamy state of sleep. When I awakened, the water had cooled down considerably, so I quickly stepped out and wrapped a big, fluffy towel around me. I put on a pair of comfortable pajamas and crawled into bed. Listening to the rhythmical ticking of the clock on my nightstand and the occasional sound of the wind in the leaves of the tree near the window, I fell into a peaceful sleep.

* * * * * * *

It was Sunday morning and I awakened refreshed and ready for the new day. I had already gotten up, made coffee and fixed a light breakfast. As I sat there drinking my coffee, the phone rang.

It was Billy. He said that he was just checking in with me and told me that he missed me very much. He said that a multitude of meetings had kept him tied up frequently since he'd been in Los Angeles and that it was too late to call when he got out of them. He also said that he would probably be home late tomorrow evening or night.

Billy's call had lifted my spirits very little and it

had put a damper on the light-hearted mood that I had previously been in. Determined not to allow the disheartened mood that I was slipping into consume me, I decided to take solace in the fact that Billy said that he missed me and loved me. I wished that he had called me Friday night when he arrived in Los Angeles and let me know that he had gotten there safely and last night before I went to bed.

The doorbell rang, propelling me back from the depths of self-pity and loneliness. When I answered the door, there stood Sam, Dee, and Greg.

"What's up girl?" Sam said as she hugged me.

"Hey Sam…. Dee…. and Greg…. how have you been? You all come on in," I said stepping to the side and motioning them to come inside.

"Why the sad face Lynn?" Sam asked with concern in her voice.

"Oh nothing much. Billy finally got around to calling me this morning after having been in Los Angeles since Friday night. It just seems like he could have called sooner than he did. He said that he had to attend a lot of meetings and that they ran late."

"Maybe his meetings really did run late," Greg said in Billy's defense.

"Yeah right…. He should have called Friday night and let know her after he had arrived, but he didn't now did he? That was just a tad bit inconsiderate don't you think?" Sam snapped, shooting Greg a penetrating look.

Greg could only lower his head in submission because he knew deep down that Sam was right.

"Sam's right…. Billy should have called and at the least told Lynn that he'd made it safely," Dee added.

"Don't dwell on that Lynn. We came to take you to the beach. That will get you in better spirits and get you out of this house too. I'm not leaving you here to feel sorry for yourself. So go and grab a bathing suit and throw some accessories in a bag, okay? We are going to have some fun today girl."

I went into the bedroom and packed a bag and we all headed for the beach. The ride to the Isle of Palms was very nice and my spirits had already lifted. By the time we arrived at the beach, I was excited and ready for fun. The beach had tons of people everywhere.

Sam, Dee, and I grabbed our bags and headed for the dressing rooms to get changed into our bathing suits and we each had a sarong to tie around it.

Our day at the beach was off to a great start. It was a beautiful day and the moderate breeze kept the temperature at a nice comfortable level. We played volleyball, went swimming, lounged, and enjoyed strolled along the water's edge.

The Isle of Palms was a beautiful place and a great refuge from the summer heat. With six miles of white, sandy beaches, it was a place of serenity. There were slips that you could take out and enjoy South Carolina's coast, award-winning golf courses, lighted golf course and a basketball court and the beautiful beaches. Everything was here for lots of fun and relaxation.

My friends and I had a ball all day -- swimming, playing miniature golf and whatever else that appealed to us.

Before leaving our fun-filled getaway, we ate at the Morgan Creek Grill, which was located on the Isle of Palms Marina. It offered an unparalleled panoramic view of the Intracoastal Waterway and surrounding Low country marshes from waterfront dining rooms and their Upper deck Bar & Grill, on the roof of Morgan Creek Grill. They served the most wonderful seafood, steaks, chops and an array of appetizers prepared eclectic style. They also had musical entertainment that provided a lively local atmosphere.

* * * * * * *

After getting home and taking a nice relaxing bath, I got ready for bed. I had checked the answering machine, when I first arrived home and there was no message from Billy. He had not called my cell phone either and this seemed strange and caused me great concern. I didn't want to dwell on the fact that he had not called me because it would only cause me more apprehension -- so I tried to convince myself to let it go and just went to bed. Though I felt much loneliness and dismay, I did manage to fall asleep.

Chapter

SEVEN

When I slowly awakened this morning and looked over at the clock, it was a little past four. A small breeze stirred the curtains from a slightly open window. The leaves of the magnolia tree outside the window moved slowly back and forth. I followed their movements with my eyes as I lay half between waking and sleeping. They lulled me back into a sound sleep. The next time I looked at the clock, it was five thirty.

I jumped up, showered and dressed. I was in the kitchen at five minutes to six making coffee. A few minutes later, Billy came in and poured him a cup of coffee. I had mixed up some waffle batter and poured some in the waffle iron and closed it. I put on some grits and placed some ham in the skillet. After taking a fork and moving the ham around in the skillet, I prepared and scrambled some eggs. I placed ham, eggs, and grits in our plates, and then removed the waffles from the waffle iron and put them in additional saucers along with peach butter and waffle syrup.

Billy and I chatted as we ate; talking about what we each thought our day would be like.

Billy pushed his chair back from the table as he placed the last bite of food in his mouth.

"Got to go honey…. Breakfast was great," he said, leaning down to kiss me.

Billy quickly strode out of the kitchen and picked up his briefcase that was sitting next to the kitchen doorway.

"See you this evening Lynnie," he yelled back, as he walked out the front door.

I finished eating and cleared the table. After washing the dishes, I decided to leisurely drink another cup of coffee, as I mentally mapped out my schedule for today. I figured that I would work on the quilt for a few hours today, and then maybe do a little window-shopping at the mall. It sounded like a plan to me.

I had been working on the quilt for a while when a familiar thought came across my mind.

One day that I was sewing, the notion to go back to school invaded my mind again. I tried to dismiss the thought, but it kept nagging at me. It had been over a year and a half since Billy and I married and he has been doing extremely well at work. I felt it should be okay to go back to school now. So I decided that I would talk to Billy when he got home that evening. I was preparing a special meal for him in hopes of enlightening the evening. Looking over at the big grandfather clock I noticed it was almost time for Billy to come home. As I set the table, I hummed a merry tune. I loved cooking for Billy and trying to be a great wife. As I worked in the kitchen, thoughts of my grandmother and how grateful I was for her making me learn how to cook invaded my mind. I had been so much of an outdoors person and enjoyed flowers and nature. My thoughts were interrupted by the front door closing.

"Baby doll, I'm home!" Billy called out.

"I'm in the kitchen honey!" I answered in a whimsical tone.

"Um-m-m! Something really smells good!"

Billy walked into the kitchen, put his arms around me and pulled me to him.

"Lynnie, you take such good care of me. I don't know what I would ever do without you," he said softly. "You're the best!"

"Let's hope you won't ever have to find out," I said, smiling mischievously.

Billy kissed me lightly on the lips and turned and

made a beeline for the fridge. He got out a beer and popped the top while I finished setting the table.

"So …. what's on the menu this evening, Babe?"

"Your favorite meal, hot pepper steak, mashed potatoes, candied yams, and home-made dinner rolls. I also made your favorite pie…. lemon icebox."

"Oh yes…. let me get washed up and I'll be back in a flash."

Billy brushed my lips lightly with his, gave me a quick wink and a mischievous look before he disappearing down the hall.

While he was gone, I sat down at the table and reflected for moment on how Billy thought that I was the best. I really had been a good wife to him and he had hot meals and a clean home to come to each and every day. He got massages after he has had stressful days at the office and I listened attentively while he raved about his colleagues. I did whatever I could to make his life as comfortable for him as possible. I waited on him hand and foot because I loved him so much. But I wondered now would he be willing to compromise for me. Suddenly, I felt Billy's arms sliding around my waist and he began planting a trail of sensuous kisses along my neck. I very smoothly maneuvered out of his grasp and turned around to face him.

"You naughty thing," I said shaking my finger at him while displaying a fake frown. "You sit yourself down here so that I can give you your supper," I playfully scolded.

Billy obeyed my orders and seated himself at the table, while I served his meal. I fixed a plate for myself and sit down at the table across from Billy. We ate while he talked about his day at work. I responded and listened attentively as he rambled on and on about things that that were often senseless at times. I had always paid attention to Billy's every word and gave him the assurance I felt that he craved.

My longing to go back to school had somehow embedded itself in my mind and I couldn't break free of its existence. For the first time since we married, my mind had never wandered off in the midst of his elaborate conversation. I wondered why Billy never asked about any interests of mine. Our conversations were always about him and about what he wanted. Though I was proud of him and of the things he has accomplished, I did want to be able to be successful in the career I had chosen for myself. I wanted to be something other than a housewife. Billy and I had agreed to put off my finishing college for about a year, but the plan was not to be put on hold indefinitely.

"Lynnie, dinner was great!" Billy exclaimed, placing the last spoonful in his mouth, and breaking my train of thought.

"Thanks honey!" "Are you ready for dessert?" I said dredging up a smile.

"I can't wait. How about a nice thick slice, okay sweetheart?"

"Coming right up," I answered getting up from the table.

While I was slicing the pie, I decided that now was the time to ask him how he felt about me going back to school. I placed each of us a slice of pie in a saucer and returned to the table. "Here you go," I said whimsically.

Billy dove right in and I seated myself in a chair next to him.

"Billy, how would you feel about me going back to school? It's been over a year now since you begun your job and you are doing really well."

Billy stopped eating and his face showed a mass of bewilderment.

I swallowed hard, and continued to go with my thoughts.

"I would go part-time so that I could still cook for you and take care of our home," I pleaded.

Billy's facial expression softened a little.

"Lynnie, honey, I thought that you had changed your mind about going back to school. I assumed that you wanted to start a family -- I know I do. I want to have children with you baby."

"But Billy, I -- I -- uh – uh---

"Don't you love me enough to have kids with me," he blurted out, interrupting me. "I love you Lynnie --- so damn much! Don't you want kids?" I want you to be mother to our kids. Come on, let's start a family."

Billy rose up from the table, with his intoxicating eyes gazing into mine and took me by both hands. His touch sent a warm sensation through me, as I began to go into meltdown. With feelings of desire and passion slowly consuming me, it was very hard for me to stand firm on our earlier discussion of me going back to school. Though my mind was in turmoil with the things Billy had just dropped on me, I still wanted to try to plead my case about school.

"Oh Billy, I – I -- still want --

Billy brought his lips down on mine muffling my shaky voice. As he parted my lips and his tongue darted aimlessly about my mouth, I fell victim to his moist sweetness. Billy pulled me closer and began caressing my now trembling body, starting at my shoulders and working his way down the curve of my lower back. His hands sent a raging warmth down to my loins, as I surrendered, totally in his mercy. Billy released his claim on my lips and looked deeply into my eyes. Being so close to him and looking into those dark, brown mesmerizing eyes of his, I caved in to his wishes. I loved him and would do just about anything to please him.

"The things one does in the name of love. Okay --- I give up --- let's start a family," I uttered softly.

Billy's eyes lit up like a kid who just got a new toy he always wanted. He lifted me off the floor by my waist and spun around with me several times before placing me back on the floor. Then he planted such a smothering kiss on me that I melted into his arms.

* * * * * * *

The next morning, it was back to the same old routine and I made Billy breakfast before he rushed off to work. I went about my chores tidying up and doing the laundry while humming a familiar tune. But this particular morning was different for me because I was elated for having made my husband such a happy man. God knows that I love children and one-day hope to be blessed with them. But having children could have been postponed until a little later. After seeing Billy's reaction to his proposal of starting a family right away, made me feel that I had made the right choice.

* * * * * * *

A few months after making the decision to start a family, I was sitting at the kitchen table sipping on my third cup of coffee. I stood up to get a bagel and felt such an overwhelming dizziness that I stumbled. Grabbing the back of a chair in front of me, I steadied myself until the dizziness passed. As I stood there gathering my composure, a thought invaded my mind about how I had been feeling so odd lately. My cycle was late this month too --- about two weeks, and I have never been late. When I was that the dizziness had passed and the nauseated feeling let up, I began cleaning up the kitchen. You know, you could be pregnant, my subconscious mind told me, as the tone echoed through my very existence.

I decided to go to the doctor in order to pacify my mind. So I finished doing the dishes and left them to drain, while I darted off to shower and dress for my visit to the doctor's office.

Once there, the doctor confirmed my suspicions.

"You're going to be a mommy Mrs. Matthews," Dr. Balthrop said with a big smile. "Congratulations!"

Dr. Balthrop told me to get dressed and said that he would be waiting in his office to discuss the proper diet and other pertinent information mothers-to-be need to know.

I smiled nervously and agreed.

While dressing, I only thought of Billy and how thrilled he would be of the news that I was carrying his child. Though I had mixed feelings, I couldn't wait to share the news with him.

On the way home, I silently reviewed everything Dr. Balthrop had said. Throughout my pregnancy, I knew that I had to make sure that I ate a healthy diet if I wanted our baby to have a good start.

When I got home, I prepared a romantic dinner for the two of us. Everything had to be perfect when I told Billy the good news.

Billy was on time as usual and I was waiting for him. The room was dimly lit and the candle's flames swayed ever so gently.

"Billy, Honey, stay right there. I'll be out in a second," I yelled from the kitchen. "Just sit and relax on the sofa."

Billy loosened his tie and sat down.

"What are you up to in there woman," he said in a suspicious tone.

Billy had noticed the wine on ice in the ice bucket.

"So, what's the occasion, baby? What are we celebrating?"

Just then, I emerged with two wine glasses and dressed in the most provocative way.

Billy was in absolute awn, as he stared at me. The look on his face told me that he was pleased with my selection. For a moment, Billy's lips only moved, but no words were uttered.

"Ly – Ly – Lynnie, you are so beautiful," he stammered.

Handing him a wine glass, I graciously slid up beside him on the sofa. Very softly, I outlined his face with feathery, sensuous kisses, while staring seductively into his soft, dark eyes.

"Billy --- Sweetie --- we're going to have a baby," I uttered softly.

His eyes widened and his masculine face eased into an enormous smile.

"Baby --- You're pregnant --- I'm going to be a father!"

Billy slowly rose from this seat, sits his wine glass on the coffee table, and clasped his hands together.

"I'm going to be a father!"

Billy took my wine glass and sits it on the coffee table.

Suddenly, he grabs me, pulling me into his arms.

Lynnie --- Baby ---You have made me so happy! I love you! I love you!" Billy shouted over and over, as he squeezed me so tightly.

Billy released his hold on me slightly to look into my eyes, and then he gently kissed my eager lips. I felt a hot, searing sensation ripping through my body. As his lips became more urgent, mine responded equally. I parted my lips to allow him easy access to delight the innermost depths and recesses, as my tongue danced with his enthusiastically. His hands slipped inside my camisole, as experienced fingers urged my nipples to stiffened peaks. We seemed to simultaneously drift to the floor, as our passion and desires soared out of control. Our breathing quickened, as we united and our rhythm escalated. Meeting each other stoke for stroke, we maintained our fiery, sensual love dance until we reached the ultimate ecstasy. As we gripped each other tightly, our climax was like the fury of an erupting volcano spewing hot, molten lava.

As we lay drenched in our blissful aftermath, Billy holds me closely. Now, I feel as though this pregnancy will bond us even closer. I silently wish that this closeness

Billy and I have and the security that I feel at this very moment, would last us forever.

EIGHT

During the first few months of my pregnancy, Billy was as happy as a lark. The idea of becoming a father just seemed to do strange things to him and I really didn't know whether or not this was the expected norm for a father-to-be. The prospect of our new arrival had Billy so upbeat and cheerful and it made me happy to see him that way. He brought me surprises on a regular basis and bought cute, little stuffed animals --- and big ones for the baby's room. I busied myself with decorating the room with colorful wallpaper and beautiful furniture. These past months were happy times and I had a wonderful husband who loved me. After all, I was carrying our love child.

Later that evening, Billy didn't come home at his usual time of 5 p.m. He's usually pretty punctual, but it was almost 7:30 and I had not received a call nor had he made it home. I became concerned because this was out of his character. I phoned his job, but got no answer. I also called his cell phone, but only got his voice mail. I wondered where could he be.

Around 9 p.m., I heard a car pull into the drive followed by a door closing. Within minutes, Billy was coming through the front door.

"Hi Honey…. is everything okay? You are so late that I thought something had happened to you."

"I…. I'm fine…. Just fine Lynn. I just had to work over for a bit," Billy stammered.

"I called you at work, but got no answer."

"I was in and out of the office…. Probably just missed me."

"Look…. Ly…. Lynn. I…. I'm really tired okay," he said stumbling toward the bedroom.

"Billy…. don't you want to eat? I have supper ready," I called after him.

Billy only mumbled back and disappeared into the bedroom. I stood there confused, not knowing nor understanding what had just happened. Walking over to the sofa, I sat down, trying to make sense of things. I wondered why Billy was acting so strangely. None of what he has said made much sense to me. He has never done anything like this before. Maybe Billy had been working late and was tired. He has not lied to me before, so I should not have any doubts about my husband.

Deciding to dismiss my restless thoughts about the incident, I went to check on Billy. When I got to the bedroom, I found him flopped across the bed and he had gone sound asleep. I pulled off his shoes and threw a comforter over him. I got another comforter from the closet and returned to the living room, where I got comfortable on the sofa. I turned on the T.V. and flipped through the channels until I found some old Sanford & Son reruns. Curling up on the sofa, I watched T.V. until I fell asleep.

When I awakened the next morning, Billy had gotten up and was gone for work without even saying good-bye. I was a little disappointed at first that I didn't get to see him, but decided not to dwell on it. Instead, I chose to put on some coffee and make myself a light breakfast.

After breakfast, I cleaned up the kitchen, and then made up the bed. I finished up the rest of my daily chores and went for a walk in the park.

It was a beautiful day out and the trees swayed gracefully in the moderate, scented wind. When I arrived at the park, it was just as beautiful. There were quite a few people sprinkled about, some of them jogging, some were strolling, and some of them were having picnics. It was just a lovely day for whatever your pleasure might have been. I couldn't leave the park before visiting my favorite area, the duck pond with the arched walkway over it. There were scores of ducks and swans swimming about that people were feeding.

When I left the park, I had a few errands to run and then stop by the store to pick up a few items for supper. I wanted Billy to have a good, hot meal when he got home.

It had come to be late afternoon by the time I made it home. As I entered the door, the phone was ringing, so I rushed to answer it. I thought that it might have been Billy checking in with me.

"Hello girlfriend…. What are you doing?" the familiar voice said.

"Sam…. Is this you?" I asked, in an uncertain tone.

"Of course Lynnie…. don't you recognize my voice?"

I sort of thought that it was you, but I just couldn't quite catch your voice. I knew that the voice seemed familiar to me."

"How have you been?" Sam asked.

"I've been doing okay, but I am a little concerned about Billy. He's been acting a little strange. He came home late last night with the strangest look on his face and he was acting just as strange."

"Well…. You know I think that your husband is strange anyway, but that's just my opinion."

"I know Sam that he doesn't be very nice toward you and Dee and I don't understand why he acts like that either. He won't even try to get to know either of you."

"I think he wants to isolate you from having any interests in anything other than him," Sam said sarcastically.

"I really hate to believe that Billy is that selfish."

"In time Lynnie I believe that his true colors will come out…. Mark my words," Sam warned.

"Lynnie…. Look…. I got to go. I just called to see how you were. If you need anything or just want to hang out, give me a ring okay?"

"Sure Sam, and thanks for calling…. Take care."

Sam's harsh words about Billy lashed at my mind. Billy just can't be that self-centered I thought. It's probably just the pressures of his job.

Dismissing Sam's words from my mind, I started preparing supper. I knew that Billy was due to be home in a couple of hours and I wanted him to have a good, hot meal.

It had come to be 5 p.m. and there was no Billy. My mind drifted back to last night and the way Billy acted when he came home. Maybe he is working late again, I told myself, but he will be here.

After a few hours had passed and there was no sign of Billy, I tried phoning him at work. But just like last night, I got no answer. Just as I was going to try the call again,

I heard a car door slam. Shortly afterwards, Billy walked through the door.

"Billy…. Hi…. what happened? I was just getting ready to try calling you again."

Billy gave me a penetrating stare. His eyes had that same glossy appearance as they did last night. His eyes made erratic movements, as he came near me.

"Why…. Why were you calling my job…? You checking up on me now."

"I was only concerned Billy. You usually are never late."

"Yea…. Yeah right. You expect me to believe that you were just worried. You…. You just don't trust me do you?"

"Oh Billy…. you know that's not true. I do trust you and I also love you…. I love you very much. You just hadn't been coming home this late before."

"No-o-o-o! You…. You're trying to spy on me. Yeah…. That's…. that's what's going…. going on."

Billy stammered so badly and displayed a crazed, wild look on his face. God…. What is wrong with my husband I thought? Billy had started pacing back and forth and muttering partial words and sentences. His odd behavior was scaring me and making me very uneasy.

Suddenly, Billy stopped pacing and stared at me as though he was looking into my soul. I started to speak.

"Billy I…."

My words were cut short by a blow across the face from the back of Billy's hand, knocking me across the sofa.

The blow was so hard that my eye felt as if it was going to explode. I lay there and looked up at Billy in fear and in absolute shock. I never thought that Billy would ever hit me.

Then, as if someone had dashed ice-cold water over him, Billy just stared at me wide-eyed…. as if trying to comprehend what he had just done.

"Oh…. Oh my God! Ly…. Lynnie! I…. I'm so sorry," Billy said, dropping to his knees beside me.

"I…. I can't believe I just did that. I…. I don't know what came over me Lynnie."

Billy grabbed me abruptly, pulling me into arms. He rocked me as if he were rocking a baby and just kept apologizing over and over.

When Billy stopped rocking me, he looked deeply into my eyes as he stroked my face.

I…. I'm really am sorry sweetheart. Forgive me…. please. I…. I've just been so tired and stressed out honey. I didn't mean to…. to hurt you," He said apologetically.

As I looked at Billy, my heart went out to him and my fear dissipated. I placed my hand gently on his face, stroking it lovingly.

"I know that you didn't intend to hurt me sweetheart and I do forgive you. I know how stressing your job can be."

"I promise that…. that I will not do this again."

"I know Billy…. I know."

I sat there with Billy briefly, holding his hands in mine. Looking into his eyes, I knew that I couldn't hold this freak incident against him. I truly believed that he didn't mean to hurt me.

"Come on Billy," I said, pulling him up off the sofa. "Let me fix you something to eat."

Billy smiled a crooked smile at me, as a relieved look seemed to wash over his face.

After we ate supper, Billy and I got ready for bed. We showered together, each taking turns soaping each other down. Our shower together was very enjoyable…. kind of like old times.

When we got into bed, Billy pulled me closely and tightly into his arms. This is the Billy that I remember…. loving and caring.

As I lay in Billy's arms, I remembered the incident from earlier that night. He really wasn't himself and I don't know what could have come over him. I guess the stress of the job was getting to him more than I thought. I did believe that he was sorry for hitting me, so I'm not going to dwell on that anymore.

I turned over to look at Billy. He had fallen asleep because I could hear his steady, easy breathing. I turned back over and snuggled in closer to my husband and fell asleep too…. content to be in his arms and have his love.

Chapter

NINE

July had approached and Billy and I seemed to be on an even slightly more keel, at least, so I chose to believe in my mind. Billy would still get edgy at times, but I'm sure that his job was the culprit. Sam's warnings about Billy still lurked in the shadows of my mind about his true colors eventually coming out. I knew that Sam meant well by the things she said against my husband, but I just couldn't accept her beliefs. I believe that my cheerfulness and optimistic attitude will see Billy and me through whatever ordeal that could arise. I believe that I can help Billy see that life should be happy and he can be content. I was Billy's loving, devoted wife and I can always forgive his actions because I love him. Sometimes my gut feelings would try to signal me about Billy's ways and actions, but I never allowed those feelings to fully materialize. It would be wrong and unbecoming of a good wife I thought, if I didn't believe in my husband and try to please him. I simply denied the feelings and let Billy do whatever made him content. I loved Billy beyond reason and it didn't matter what he did, I would always end up forgiving him. I was totally devoted to keeping my marriage together at all costs.

Billy's company threw a big company picnic each year during the 4th of July. It was a way for the employees and their families to get together and to get better acquainted. When Billy came home that night, he spoke to me about it.

"Uhhhh.... Lynn.... The company is having their annual company picnic this Friday. I'm supposed to invite you to come. Now.... Uh.... You don't have to come if you don't want to. Do you want to come," he asked, not appearing very enthused or showing very much emotion.

"Yes.... I will go Billy," I replied happily.

"Fine.... Well.... The picnic starts around noon."

"I'll be there with bells on."

The few days before the picnic passed rather quickly and Friday had arrived. Billy arose and left without waking me this morning. When I woke up, I went on and did my usual chores so that I would have time to shower and dress and make the picnic.

When I finished my chores, there were a couple of hours left before the picnic was due to start. I showered and changed and headed for the picnic.

As I drove, my mind went back to how Billy had asked me to come to the picnic. It was as if he was secretly hoping that I wouldn't want to go and that he only asked me because it was expected of him.

When I arrived on Billy's job, the festivities were in full swing. There were lots of people and they all seemed to be having a great time. As I slowly walked through the maze of unfamiliar faces, I tried to be upbeat and not appear as nervous and as out of place as I felt. Many of the people there were very friendly. These people's friendliness was the one thing that helped me to relax a little.

Finally, I spotted Billy over in a somewhat secluded area of the grounds chatting with a woman. As I approached them, their conversation appeared to be intimate because of the way she would laugh and touch Billy. They were so wrapped up in their conversation that they barely noticed my approach.

"Hi Billy," I said, trying to appear cheerful.

"Oh…. Oh Lynnie…. Hi," Billy said nervously, looking as though he had just been caught stealing.

"Did you just get here?"

"Well…. I've been here for a bit," I said, eyeing this woman.

"Oh…. Lynn…. This is Brenda…. Brenda Sims. She works in our accounting department," Billy explained.

Brenda was just standing there with a stupid looking smirk on her face that I really didn't appreciate. She didn't look much like anyone that would work in accounting to me. As a matter of fact, she didn't have a professional appearance at all, even if she had been dressed in a suit. She looked thin and didn't appear to take much consideration to her personal hygiene either. She just wasn't a very attractive person.

"I'm pleased to meet you Brenda. I'm Billy's wife," I said, extending my hand.

"I know…. I know who you are. Billy has told me so much about you."

"Brenda…. Look…. I'll catch you later to discuss that accounting issue some more, okay," Billy said.

"Come on Lynnie…. let me introduce you to the company president and the vice president," Billy said, pulling me by my arm.

"Nice meeting you Brenda," I said, as Billy was pulling me away.

Billy introduced me around to a few of his colleagues and the president of the company. Then Billy helped me fix a plate and seated me next to a homely looking guy he had introduced me to earlier. His name was Ben and he loved talking. Billy got me seated near Ben and told me that he would be right back. He mumbled something about speaking to the company CEO about some type of engineering matter.

In the meantime, I was left trying to make small talk with Ben, who was talking almost non-stop. Gosh…. The guy barely took time to catch his breath, before rambling on.

I had finished my meal and was getting tired of listening to Ben. I wondered what had happened to Billy. He had been gone for quite a while and I had not seen him.

I managed somehow, to get away from Ben and begin my search for Billy. As I strolled over the grounds admiring the landscaping, I stopped momentarily to chat with some of the people. It was a very lovely day and a nice breeze was blowing…. just strong enough to cause my hair to gently flow in harmony.

After all of the walking I had done in search of Billy, nature was calling and I needed to find a bathroom. I finally spotted the restroom just ahead of me a short distance. On the way to the bathroom, I walked past a small pond that was surrounded by beautiful magnolias and lilacs. There also was a small bridge that arched over the middle of the pound. I stood there for a moment admiring this lovely vision and taking in the smell of the fragrant blossoms.

Just as I was about to leave, I saw Billy and Brenda standing near the pond, but on the other side. I watched, as Brenda reached out and took Billy's hand. Then she pulled his arm around her, as she stepped in closer to him.

Billy didn't appear to be putting up much of a resistance to her advances. As I watched this woman coming on to my husband, an achy lump formed in my throat. My eyes filled with tears and my stomach felt as though it were being tied up in knots.

Suddenly, Brenda threw her arms around Billy and hugged and kissed him passionately and he seemed to eagerly respond with no resistance.

As I stood there in total shock and disbelief of what I was witnessing, Billy looked up and noticed that I was standing there. He immediately broke Brenda's embrace and stepped away from her.

I turned to leave because I had seen enough of their idle display of affection. I rushed to the bathroom and quickly closed the door behind me. Once inside, the tears flooded my eyes. It hurt so badly to see Billy that intimate with another woman.

I stayed in the bathroom until I got my bearings and until I thought Billy was not nearby. When I felt that the coast was clear, I slowly eased the bathroom door open and evaluated outside. Feeling confident that no one was there, I made a mad dash for the car. As I weaved my way through the maze of people, I could see my car. When I reached the car, I hopped in and sped away.

On my drive home, I replayed Billy and Brenda's liaison. I mad me sick to think that Billy would allow her to hang all over him like that.

When I got home, all I wanted to do was take a long, hot soak and try to forget about everything. My body was so tense and I needed to loosen up. I drew a full tub bath and added my favorite scented oil, and slowly slipped in the silky, fragrant water. I closed my eyes and allowed my head to rest on the bath pillow. I wanted to soak away all of my pain and tension. My body succumbed to the heated water and began to loosen up. My body loosened up so much that I dozed off for a few minutes.

When I awakened, I felt so much more relaxed, that I decided that it was time to get out of the tub. I dried off and threw on a big, loose caftan and went out into the living room.

As I reached the living room, I suddenly felt movement in my stomach. I had just reached my third month of pregnancy and this was the first movement I had noticed. The fluttering feeling was so strange, but nice…. It excited me. I was thrilled to feel the movement of my baby. As I placed my hand on my stomach, I felt another flutter. It was such an amazing thing…. to feel the new life that stirred within me…. it was an indescribable experience.

As I sat down on the sofa, Billy walked through the door. Just seeing him brought back the pain he and Brenda had caused me.

"Why did you run off like that today Lynn? I looked for you for hours until I finally noticed that your car was gone."

I looked at Billy dumb-founded, trying to think of what to say and how I would say it. It was apparent that he was angry by the expression on his face and the tone of his voice.

"I saw you and Brenda out near the pond. The two of you looked pretty cozy and I saw her hug you," I said in an unstable voice.

"Lynn…. All I was doing was trying to console her because she has been going through a rough time of it lately. I just let her cry on my shoulder."

"What about my feelings and needs Billy. You just went off and left me alone and you didn't return. I could use some of that compassion that you were giving so freely to her."

Billy flashed a gaze of contempt at me.

"What's the point of trying to discuss this with you anyway? You could fucking care less about what I was trying to do.

Billy stormed out of the room. Within a few minutes, he was back carrying suitcase.

"Look Lynnie…. I have a business trip to make to Atlanta. I'll see you in a couple of days.

Then Billy just walked out without so much of a hug or a good-bye.

Long after Billy had gone, I sat on the sofa…. pondering, trying to make sense of something that just didn't make any sense to me. Billy's walking out as he had done, was so much of like a slap in the face and it hurt so badly that I was practically numbed. How insensitive and disrespectful his leaving had been I told myself.

Sam's words haunted me now…. Especially the things she had said about Billy's true colors coming out. In my mind, my husband just couldn't be that cruel. Billy is just misunderstood…. I must have done something wrong…. It had to be me. That's what it is…. It's me. All I have to do to fix it is to be a more devoted, loving wife…. Don't place any limits on him to add to his stress. If I do all the things that a *good* wife should, I believe that Billy will come around.

Over-riding my initial thoughts of standing my ground with Billy, I told myself to just allow him to have his way…. that it all will work out.

Chapter

TEN

September was dawning and the leaves were turning to their magnificent orange, yellow and golden fall colors. I would have to wait now until next year to experience the wonderful fragrances of the magnolias and lilacs. I wasn't too sad about the changing season though because the fall of the year had its' own marvelous and brilliant contributions to offer.

I had nearly reached my fourth month of pregnancy. My baby has been very active…. kicking, moving around, and stretching. I talked to my baby often now. During some of the baby's active periods, I would place a saucer on my stomach and watch it move about.

The few times that allowed myself to think, I remembered certain things about how I had grown up. I had never known the kind of anger that Billy projects at me. I never experienced his kind of anger when I was growing up. My home had been full of laughter and love…. Family squabbles that ended almost as soon as they began.

As time went on, Billy still got angry and would scream terrible things at me that left me shaking and frightened. Since Billy has been being angry with me more and more, I must be doing something very wrong. I know that after Billy and I have a fight or an argument, he would apologize to me later and tell me how sorry he had been to lose his temper. Then he would tell me that if I only did things the right way and did what was expected of me, he would not be forced to get angry with me. So I decided that I just wouldn't allow his anger to discourage me from being a good wife and mother-to-be.

Billy started to go on more overnight business trips more regular. But I knew that his job required him to do this…. that it was necessary. Billy would give me a call in advance and tell me that he would not be coming home on those nights he had to go out of town.

One evening, Billy didn't arrive home at the time that he usually does. Several hours had gone by and he hadn't called me to let me know whether or not he would be home. I put his supper back into the oven, set the dial to warm and decided that maybe he had a late meeting or some sort of a problem at the site. In order to try to relieve some of the anxiety of Billy's unusual lateness, decided to take relaxing bath. A long, hot soak always seemed to calm me whenever I was stressed.

The bath did work its magic and I had a much better perspective than before. Feeling much calmer and relaxed, I put on some jazz and began humming to the music. Curling up on the sofa, my mind drifted back to Billy. Why haven't I heard anything from him -- why hasn't he called I thought.

The calm, relaxed atmosphere was broken by the sound of loud, screeching tires followed by a car door slamming. Just as I stood up and started toward the front door, Billy charged in with a rather strained look on his face.

"Hi Honey," I said concerned and puzzled. "I was beginning to worry about you. What happened to you? I expected you hours ago. Is everything okay?"

Billy was still looking a bit strange and I was a little timid because I had never seen him this way before.

"I had a consultation with some of my colleagues," he replied in a sort of harsh, elevated tone.

"Why didn't you call me sweetheart? You know that I would worry about you. You're usually always home by five o'clock --- and – and -- I've been worrying about you all this time."

Billy's face changed abruptly. His eyes had a kind of glazed appearance and seemed to move about erratically. This image of Billy had started to really frighten me.

"What in the hell is this --- the fucking third degree? What's your damn problem? You think I'm fucking lying or something?"

"Oh – no –no Billy, I – I – didn't think anything like that sweetie. I just wandered wha --."

With the back of his hand, Billy drew back and hit me across the face, knocking me to the floor. A piercing pain shot through my eye that felt like it would explode and my head felt as if it were spinning around. There was a short silence for a moment, as I tried to lift myself upon my knees. I slowly gazed up at Billy, who was just standing there with his mouth open and looking dumb-founded.

Momentarily, Billy realized what he'd done and a shroud of shock flushed over his face. He helped me to my feet as seemed to struggle with his own stability. Trying to steady myself, I stared at this man who I love with all my heart --- never thinking nor believing he would ever hurt me.

"I—I—I—I'm sorry Lynnie, I'm so sorry---My God! What have I done?" He replied trying to console me.

"Lynnie, Honey, I swear---I'll never hit you again. I just don't know what came over me. The last thing I want to do is hurt you or our baby. I love you, I really do." Billy pleaded.

Billy pulled me into his arms and held me tightly, trying to comfort me. Still feeling a little light-headed and confused from all that's happened, I didn't put out much effort to resist Billy's caress. I was still very much shaken, but the words he said and the way he held me made me feel he was genuinely sorry. I truly believed that he was sorry for hitting me. My pushing against Billy slightly caused him to loosen his tight hold on me. Looking into his handsome face now I could see that it showed much sympathy and regret.

"Billy--you know now that was only worried about you when I asked what had happened. I trust you--I always have and with all my heart. But you hurt me and there was no real reason for that. You could have caused injury to our child," I said with concern.

Billy took my hand and led me over to the sofa, coaxing me to sit down by him.

"I know Honey--and I promise you, this won't ever happen again. This job just gets me so stressed out sometimes and it's so demanding. I've been trying to get this project off the ground. But that is not excuse for hitting you the way I did and coming home and taking it out on you. Please forgive me, Lynnie--please."

Looking into his dark eyes, I gently rubbed solemn face.

"I love you Billy--of course, I forgive you. I understand that work can stress you out and that you would never intentionally hurt me," I said reassuringly. "Let's try to put this behind us and go on, okay?"

Billy and I both agreed that this was best forgotten and that we would go on with our lives together--forgive and forget. Though I did agree to forgive and forget this incident, in my innermost psyche, I still wondered what had come over Billy. What had caused this sort of violent temperament? What possessed him to be so vile and inconsiderate? What is happening to my loving, gentle, and caring husband?

After yesterday's incident, my face was a little sore. My right eye was swollen and I had a somewhat noticeable bruise, so I began applying cold compresses. Since Billy had already left for work, I lay on the sofa and held the compress to my sore face for a while. The thought of Billy's actions last night crept back in my mind. I envisioned the crazed look that had dominated his handsome face.

"Oh just put the incident out of your mind" a voice inside me urged. "You know that your husband loves you."

Deciding to follow my conscious, I allowed those bad thought to drift from my mind for I believed in Billy's words....that he did love me and that it wouldn't happen again.

The ringing doorbell brought me back to the present, as I got up to see who this could be so early this morning.

"My goodness Lynnie! What happened to you!" demanded Sam, frowning.

And Dee, whose face showed genuine concern added, "Yeah ….your eye is swollen and your fa…."

Breaking in on Dee's statement, I interrupted saying, "Oh….it's nothing….really. Come on in," I invited.

Sam and Dee followed me inside and seated themselves as they displayed their anticipation of my real explanation about my swollen eye and bruised face.

"Well-l-l-l-l-l! Aren't you going to tell us?" Sam remarked impatiently.

"All right…. all right already!" responding in a slightly annoyed manner. "You see…. I was trying to open one of those overhead cabinet doors in the kitchen….and it was stuck….I just pulled a little too hard and it hit me."

Sam and Dee's worried looks seemed to dissolve away as they became more relaxed about what I had told them. They seemed to believe the lie that I just told them.

"Girl….I'm sure am glad that's what really happened….I was worried at first that Billy might have done that," Sam said smiling uneasily. "Hey….I'm sorry Lynnie for even thinking that Billy could do something like that. After all, I really don't know him well enough to judge him like that. I hope that we can still be friends"

"Why of course we can…. no harm was done," I said, reaching out to hug my friend.

Dee smiled at Sam and me approvingly and added, "Now that we got all the formalities out of the way, we can get down to the business at hand….going shopping!"

Sam and I both exchanged glances as if we read each other's mind and decided to throw pillows at Dee.

After our pillow fight, I showered and dressed, pausing momentarily at the full-length mirror on my closet door. Turning from side to side, I tried to see if I was starting to show. I still had almost a washboard stomach at 4 months into the pregnancy. Just a slight bulge that was barely noticeable told the tell-tale signs of my pregnancy

"Hey Lynnie! It would be great if you could make it out of there in this cen-tu-ry!" Dee yelled out impatiently.

"Yeah girl…. come on…. we have a lot of stores to hit…. get a move on it," Sam added.

"Okay! Okay! I'm coming right out you guys! I yelled back.

After giving my face a final check-up to make sure I had concealed most of the obvious appearance of the bruise, we were off to the mall.

On the way to the mall, I admired the beautiful summer morning. It seemed particularly lovely today because I had made peace with Billy's unexpected anger and Sam's doubts about him. All was well in my world again and I looked forward to each and every day, as I counted the days until the arrival of my precious bundle of joy.

We were approaching the city, and I anticipated all the cute little baby things I would see and buy. As we coasted off 13th avenue, we searched for a parking space. Though it was early morning, the mall was busy with people going to and from the multitude of stores it contained and accommodated.

Each of us came out of the mall with a couple of bags full of goodies. Most of my purchases were for the baby, but I did find something for Billy and silently hoped that he would like it.

After our shopping spree, we were exhausted from hustling from one boutique to another. We lugged our purchases over to the dining area in mall, and ordered salads and colas. This gave us a chance to unwind and catch our breath before facing the mob of shoppers and traffic upon our departure.

After getting home with our purchases, I invited Sam and Dee to stay for a while. After telling them to make themselves at home, I went into the kitchen to start supper for Billy. He would be home in a few hours I told myself, while taking a package of steaks from the fridge. Once I had supper going, I rejoined my friends in the living room. Sam and Dee were rustling through their bags expecting their merchandise.

"Hey--do all want a drink or something," I offered, smiling at the two of them.

"Sure!" Dee nodded.

Sam, still searching through her bags, shot me a quick glance, "Me too girl! But only juice for you missy," she said, raising her brow mockingly.

"Okay--I know! I'll drink apple juice," I said whimsically.

We all sat, chatted, laughed, and enjoyed each other's companionship. In between all of our clattering and laughter, I managed to finish supper. While we all were admiring the baby things that I had purchased, Billy walked in. He looked dryly and grimly about the room, as he closed the door behind him.

"Hello Honey!" I chimed. "How was your day?"

"Hi Billy!" Sam and Dee sung in harmoniously.

With a muffled hello, Billy quickly strode off upstairs.

Sam and Dee both silently looked at each other, totally confused by Billy's behavior.

"We'd better go Lynn. Billy doesn't seem too thrilled that we're here and I really don't understand why. But we don't want to cause any problems for you," Sam spoke sternly.

"See you later Lynnie," Dee said, gathering her bags and heading for the door.

Sam warmly reached out and gathered my hands in hers.

"I'll call you Lynn, okay? You take care of yourself."

After my friends had gone, I quietly stood for a few moments trying to absorb Billy's reaction. Why was he so rude and hateful acting toward my friends I thought? Going into the kitchen, I checked on supper. Just as I began setting the table, Billy appeared in the doorway.

"I thought that I told you that I didn't want them around. They are too much of a distraction for you Lynnie!" Billy spoke in a raised tone.

"Now wait just a minute Billy…. Have I once had your supper late? No, I have not. Isn't this house always clean and orderly? Yes it is. So tell me how is me spending a little time with friends distracting me Billy?"

Showing some remorse for his hostility, Billy slowly approached me.

"You're right Lynnie…. supper is always ready and the house is always clean. I get that, really I do. But I still don't really like your friends nor do I want them around. You may like being with them so much you'll forget about me."

"Oh Billy…How am I going to forget about you? I love you. No one can take me away from you, okay?"

"I just want things to be the way they used to be…. just you and me."

"Billy…. there's room in my life for all of you," I said reassuringly, as I stepped into his arms.

Billy and I sat down and ate together and then we retired for the night. While lying in Billy's arms, my mind drifted momentarily to his comment about losing me. Where was all of this insecurity coming from? If only Billy could see inside my heart I thought. So much love resides there…. so much love…. and all of the love is for him.

Chapter

ELEVEN

A week had gone by and I had heard not one word from Sam or Dee. Billy's behavior probably had frightened them away. I really couldn't blame them if they did stay away because Billy had done nothing to make them feel as though they were welcome at our home. I had enjoyed my friends' company immensely because I was always alone when Billy was away at work. Dispirited, I got the quilt out that I had been working on in hopes that it would occupy my restless energy and thoughts. Billy had been gone for the office about an hour when the phone rang, startling me.

"Hello Lynnie, how are you?" a familiar voice echoed through the phone.

"Hello…Sam…. Oh it's so good to hear from you," I said, trying to contain my excitement. "I was just thinking of you this morning."

"Has that husband of yours calmed down? You know…. he really baffled me the last time I saw you, girl. He seems a little bit strange to me, but hey…. that's your man."

"I know that Billy does seem to act a little strange sometimes where you and Dee are concerned, but he really is a good man, Sam," I said defensively.

"Alright girl, I believe you if you say so. Who am I to try to judge him? N-E-way…. I called you to invite you to a festival they're having at the park on Friday. Dee and I are going and we wanted to see if you want to go? There will even be a live band performing."

"Sounds great Sam and I'm sure it will be a lot of fun. Tell you what…. let me get back with you later in the week, okay?"

Sure Lynnie…I'll be expecting your call. Talk to you later," Sam said in closing.

The week seemed to drag by, but I busied myself with my quilting. As I quilted, thoughts of the festival that Sam had invited me to invaded my mind and I had decided that I wanted to go. So I phoned Sam and told her that I did want to go and asked if she and Dee would pick me up.

* * * * * * *

Finally … it was Friday. I saw Billy off to work and got all of my housework done before Sam and Dee arrived that afternoon. After preparing a casserole and placing it in the oven, I set the timer to the time that I wanted it to start cooking. I also left a note for Billy just in case I made it home a little later than I had expected.

On the way to the park, we all chatted and enjoyed the beautiful summer afternoon.

"I promise you Lynn, you will have a great time…. and it will do you good to get out of the house for a while." Sam remarked. "All you do is stay up in the house."

"I'm sure we'll all have fun," I happily added.

It was 2:30 p.m. when we arrived at the park, and people had just begun gathering for the festivities. The three of us managed to pick out good spot…right under a huge sycamore tree. We spread out our blankets, pulled off our shoes, and sat down to enjoy the music. The band was already tuning up, so we hurried and got our refreshments and snacks and returned to our spot.

The band was wonderful and the late afternoon was beautiful. The moderate breeze stirring scented the air with fragrant blossoms of the many lilacs that were all about. Swallows darted about in graceful flight with their deeply forked tails.

As the festival drew to an end, some of the people had begun leaving. The sun setting cast a magnificent orange glow over the sky. Everyone who had attended had clearly enjoyed the music because they raved about great the band had been. This was the perfect end to a wonderful evening.

Sam and Dee let me out at home and I thanked them for inviting me. After promising that I would see them tomorrow, I waved good-bye. When I stepped into the house, I was a little surprised by the darkness inside. As I fumbled for the light switch, the lights suddenly popped on. There stood Billy with anger written all over his face. As he stood there looking at me, he seemed to grow angrier. He stared at me harshly and his eyes showed that glazed appearance they had displayed the last time he was angry. I swallowed hard as I watched Billy's chest heaving harder and harder and his eyes seemed to dart about uncontrollably.

"Billy…Honey…What's wrong? Why are you looking --?"

Billy backhanded me across the face.

"Oh Billy…. Please don't…please Billy…. don't," I pleaded.

When Billy raised his hand again, I shook with intense fear. I threw up my arms to try to cover my face. Billy's hand came down hard, knocking me to the floor. Quickly walking over to me, he pulled me up abruptly by my hair. Unbearable pain seared through my head, as my hair felt as though it was being pulled out from the roots. I grabbed the back of his hand to try to loosen his grip and relieve the overwhelming pain racing through my head.

"You slut…. you fucking bitch…. Where in the hell have you been? I didn't give you permission to go out or stay out for so long," Billy yelled.

"But Billy…. I didn't stay…"

Billy hit me again and I fell against the coffee table. I tried to get up, but I couldn't. This was the last thing that I remembered.

A few hours later, I awoke in a hospital bed. Through the hazy blur, I managed to focus in on Billy's face. He was at my bedside holding my hand with tears trickling down his solemn face.

"Thank God…. I thought I was going to lose you," Billy spoke in a relieved, gentle tone.

I tried to sit up, but a sharp pain that shot through my head causing me to lay back.

"Don't try to get up baby… just lie down and rest."

Just then, a tall, thin nurse entered my room that looked to be in her thirties.

"Well…. Welcome back among the living Mrs. Matthews," she said in a slightly raised voice. "My name is Vera and I'll be your nurse for tonight. Mrs. Matthews, you have a mild concussion. You will be fine and so will your baby. But we would like to keep you overnight for observation. I'll be back to check in on you a little later," the nurse said, while checking my pulse. "Can I get you anything?" she added.

"No…. no thank you…. I'm fine," I said weakly.

"Very well Mrs. Matthews…I'll see you a little later then."

After the nurse left, I said a silent prayer for my baby. I was happy that it would be okay.

"Lynnie…. I…. I'm so sorry sweetheart…really I am," Billy said, laying his head in my bosom.

"I hope that you can forgive me Lynnie. But I couldn't tell them the truth about what really happened. They would probably have me put me in jail," Billy pleaded. "I sort of lied to them…. please don't be mad. But I told them that you fell. I was so scared and I didn't know what to do," he blubbered.

He hurt me so much to see Billy cry and hurt this way, so I gently rubbed his head.

"I know Billy," I uttered softly. "But why…. why wouldn't you give me a chance to tell you where I had been? It wasn't really that late…. It was only 6 p.m. I had left you a note in case you got home before I did. I had gone to the park with Sam and Dee. We only stayed for a few hours and listened to the live band playing. Why wouldn't you give me a chance to explain, Billy?"

My throat began to throb and tears teased the corners of my eyes.

"You hurt me Billy," I choked out. "You know…. you could have injured our baby. Don't you care about our baby?" I wailed.

Billy rose up and looked at me pitifully. Tears were now streaming down my cheeks. Billy lifted me into his arms and held me lovingly.

"Lynnie…. I'm so sorry honey…I'm sorry…please forgive me one last time I beg of you. I couldn't have lived if something had happened to you or our child. If you can only see your way to forgive me this one last time," he said in a husky tone.

"I love you Billy…. and, of course, I forgive you."

I knew deep down that I loved Billy so much that I was willing to cover up the truth about what had really happened to me. So I confirmed what he had told the doctor and nurse…. that I had tripped and fallen into the coffee table.

* * * * * * *

The next morning, Billy had taken off a few hours from work to pick me up from the hospital. He was there waiting at the front desk when I arrived, flashing a huge smile and a carrying a beautiful bouquet of flowers. After seeing Billy this way made me feel as though I had made the right decision in remaining silent about what had really happened last night.

After the drive home, Billy helped me inside and made me comfortable on the sofa.

"Can I get you anything sweetie before I go to work," Billy asked attentively.

"No Billy…. I should be okay," I replied.

"I'll see you later this evening…. Don't over do it today, honey," he ordered, smiling as he exited the house.

After Billy left, I laid down on the sofa to relax for a while before trying to tackle some of my chores. While laying there, my mind traveled to a place of much confusion…. thoughts of many things Billy had said and done. Some of these things were pretty harsh and some were confusing, but they all disturbed me intensely. I wandered what was happening to the man that I loved so dearly. Who was this imposter that would mysteriously invade my Billy's persona and inspirit him into committing these awful and cruel acts to my friends and me?

Snap out of this type of thinking Lynnie, my conscience nudged. You know that you promised to love this man for better or for worst. He's just going through a rough time right now…. You know, handling his job responsibilities, which are very demanding.

I sit up slowly on the sofa and an overwhelming feeling inched through me.

"I do love you Billy," I spoke aloud, as if trying to force my mind into acceptance of the idea.

I decided that I would go up to our bedroom and start straightening up there first. I figured that it probably looked like a disaster area since I wasn't here this morning to simplify his attire.

As I had presumed, the room was a mess with clothes thrown everywhere. Billy's blazer was thrown over the back of a chair, so I picked it up to place it on a hanger. Checking his pockets as I usually did before taking his clothes to the cleaners, I found an envelope that had been folded several times. I took the envelope and unfolded and felt something hard in it like small pebbles or something. I draped the blazer back over the chair and went to the bed to sit down, still holding the envelope I had found. I lifted the flap of the envelope and peered inside, and was shaken very badly by what I saw. What I saw in the envelope looked kind of like tinted rock salt. These little pebbles turned out to be crack cocaine rocks. I was pretty certain that these were crack rocks because I had studied about drugs in my psychology class and about the effects this drug and others had on the mind. But why would Billy have such a highly addictive drug I thought.

Suddenly, I was overcome by such extreme fear that my stomach felt like it was being tied in knots. I really wanted to be in denial, but I knew better…. I knew that Billy was using dugs now. This discovery answered a lot of questions I'd had about him…. his erratic behavior and how he had been mentally and physically abusing me. But I wondered why Billy was on drugs. Nothing could be bad enough to make him turn to drugs I told myself. No matter what I did, the thought that Billy was using crack cocaine would not stray from my thoughts. I realized that I would have to confront Billy about this, but how? He had been so short-fused lately and I was certain that he would blow up on me for asking him about the drugs I had found. But I new deep down, that I would have to ask Billy about these drugs anyway, regardless of the outcome.

I walked over to the chair and picked up Billy's blazer and held it as if I were holding him. I clung to his blazer as though it was my pacifier, as I lay across our bed. Curled into a ball, I cried, because I could not understand nor could I see any justification for the drugs I had found. My head was spinning with so much confusion because I could not accept the circumstances…. This cannot be…. Not my Billy…. These thoughts echoed through my mind until I couldn't bear them anymore.

As I went back downstairs, I felt as though I were in some sort of trance. My shock and disbelief seemed to overcome my existence. I tried to divert my thoughts by throwing myself into cleaning up the house, but the thoughts always returned, haunting me endlessly.

The day had gone by in a blur and it was time to start preparing supper. After putting the finishing touches on my meatloaf, I placed it in the oven with the potatoes. Making my way to the living room, I decided to relax because it would be about an hour before supper was ready, but the doorbell rang.

When I answered the door, there stood Sam.

"Lynnie…. My God…. You look terrible! What the hell is going on?" Sam raved.

I tried to think of a good excuse, but I found myself at a lost for words.

"I…. I…. Uh-h-h…."

Sam interrupted, "Don't tell me that you hit your face on the cabinet door this time because I don't think I will believe you."

The look on my face confirmed Sam's suspicions.

"I knew it was Billy all along…. This isn't the first time he has hit you. I had a feeling that he had hit you before, but I wanted to give him the benefit of doubt…. And I wanted to maintain our friendship too."

Sam brushed by me and came on inside.

"You know what Lynnie? You're going to have to put an end to this abuse. You just can't continue to let him hurt you this way," Sam said angrily.

I closed the door and turned to face Sam. A tear flowed down my cheek as I tried to suffice the disappointment and hurt. I knew that Sam could see the hurt too because she put her arms around me.

"You know Sam …. Billy has never allowed me to have a job, so I can't just up and leave him within any viable means of support."

"Look Lynnie…. I'm your friend. If there is anything you need, you know I will help you all I can," she promised.

"You don't have to go through this alone."

"Sam…. Billy not only hits me ….. he is also using crack cocaine…. I found some in his blazer today."

Sam didn't seem to be too shocked by my news of Billy's drug use. She just reassured me that she would be there for me whenever I needed her.

Sam and I talked for a while, which helped to put me at ease a little. But she made me promise to call her anytime if I needed to…. day or night.

After Sam left, I returned to the kitchen to check on supper. Everything was ready so I set the table. When I went to get silverware, I noticed that by the wall clock, it was getting pretty late. As I placed the forks, knifes and spoons on the table, I wondered…. where was Billy?

More and more time had elapsed and I begun to get really worried. Then I heard a car door slam. As I rushed into the living room, I saw Billy staggering inside.

"Billy, thank God you're alright. I was scared to death that something had happened to you. It's been five hours since the usual time you arrive home. Why didn't you call?" I asked concerned.

Billy walked unsteadily to the sofa and plunked down.

"What's wrong with you…? Are you drunk…? High…." "Why are you so late?" I asked, becoming annoyed.

I walked over to the end table and picked up the envelope I had found earlier that day. I reached inside and pulled out its' contents and walked over to Billy, who was now standing and trying to steady himself enough to remove his jacket.

"Tell me what you are doing with these Billy," I asked extending out an open hand.

"Uh –h –h…. Lynnie…. I…. I…. we…. were just…. Uh…. Uh…. It helps me to unwind and relax," he responded in a slurred tone. Give me a break Lynnie. Me and a couple of friends…. From the office…. We…. We…. After work…. We…. We don't do much…. Then we…. Uh…. Have a few drinks."

"I would say that you had a few too many," I remarked sarcastically.

I stormed out of the room leaving him standing there looking foolish and puzzled. I went upstairs and ran myself a hot bubble bath, hoping that it would soothe away the anguish and hostility I felt for the first time toward Billy.

The bath did help, but I felt a sense of loneliness creeping into my mind. I could see now that Billy was gradually shutting me out of his life. He was turning to drugs and these friends of his for support and comfort. But why I thought…. As much as I love him and as much as I show him that I love him, how could he turn to this addictive drug and alcohol? I was slowly…. gradually losing my husband.

Chapter

TWELVE

The first rays of dawn were peeking through the vertical blinds in my bedroom when I awakened this morning. I sat up and swung my legs out of bed, as I yawned sleepily. Movement in my stomach told me that my baby had awakened also because I could feel it stretching and moving all about. I placed my hand on my stomach and rubbed it gently and softly said, "Good Morning to you sweetness."

I went to the bathroom and washed my face. As was my habit, I went to put on a pot of coffee, waited for the first cup to drip through, and took a couple of tentative sips.

I seemed to have trouble fighting off this groggy feeling this morning. I thought then that maybe some breakfast would make me feel better. So I fixed myself breakfast, which consisted of two slices of bacon, one egg, and a buttered toast with strawberry jelly.

I sipped on my coffee and only picked at my food. My appetite just wouldn't allow me to eat this morning though I knew that I should eat.

My thoughts were on Billy who had left early for work and had not awakened me. So much has been changing with my husband and I just didn't understand why.

Some of Sam's words still echoed in my mind about how selfish and manipulative Billy had been. He had been cruel to me and to my friends. Had Billy always been selfish and I just never noticed or did he grow to be this way I asked myself.

Billy had really changed on me. Where had that wonderful, lovable guy gone whom I fell in love with back in school? Where did the passionate and warm-hearted man go that I marred and had vowed to love, honor, and cherish me?

Billy had changed into someone that I didn't recognize very much anymore. He's almost like a stranger -- someone who I now only see every once in a while. The brief time that he is around he is cruel, hurtful, selfish and physically and emotionally abusive. He used to seem as though he was remorseful for hurting me. But nowadays, he seems to not care at all.

Whatever Billy is involved in cannot be good and I feel that it will catch up to him sooner or later.

Thinking back over my past life with Billy, I feel now that maybe I never really knew him -- I just thought I did. Maybe the actions that he's displaying now came from some deep-rooted problem long ago when he was growing up.

Billy came from a broken home. His mom and dad fought all the time and I can remember seeing his mom bruised up at times. His father drank a lot and stayed away from home quite often. But whenever his dad did come home, he and Billy's mom fought and argued endlessly. I remember once when I was over at Billy's house, his mom and dad were screaming and swearing at each other. I got so upset that I ran out the house and went home. My parents never acted this way so I just wasn't used to that kind of anger and fighting.

Billy's parents' fighting so much took its toll on him sometimes. It was during these tough times that Billy would be short with me. He tried to be tough and hard and not let it show that his parents' fighting got to him, but I knew that it did -- I could see it. But I never dreamed that he would end up acting this way.

Maybe Billy kept all of this bad stuff that happened between his parents suppressed so long that it festered in him. Now he is acting out his father's role with me.

I feel as though my soul is being torn in half. I love my husband and don't want to leave him. Yet a part of me can't ignore the fact that I'm pregnant, and as a mother, should protect the welfare of my unborn child from harm. Being slapped and knocked around by Billy can't be good for my baby. I can't even talk to him to try to offer my love and support. I love him, yet I'm getting more and more afraid of him.

The phone rang snapping me back to reality.

"Hello Lynn…. How are you this beautiful day?" Sam said in a raised, upbeat tone.

"Uh…. Hi Sam…. I'm okay."

"Are you sure? You don't sound okay Lynn. What's wrong?"

I guess I'm just feeling sorry for myself today. Billy got up and left this morning and didn't even say good-bye or anything," I moaned.

"I say that you need to leave the bastard. Look at how he treats you Lynn. He knocks you around and disrespects you all the time. I'm really afraid that he's going to hurt you badly one of these days."

"I get scared too sometimes Sam, but he is my husband and I still love him. Yes, he has hit me couple of times, but I don't know if he would ever hurt me badly. Besides, he always seems to be very sorry about it the times that he did hit me," I said defensively.

"I know that he's your husband Lynn, but you had better watch yourself, okay. Look…. I got to go right now, but I'll check in with you later."

The day went by in a haze. I was preparing supper not really sure if Billy would be home tonight. Since the food was practically ready, I set the temperature to low so that it would stay warm and not overcook.

I went into the living room and curled up on the sofa. I felt tired and thought that a quick nap would do me good.

Just as I had dozed off, the front door slammed, jolting me from my nap. Sitting up on the sofa, I saw Billy approaching me.

"What's wrong Billy? Why are you home so late?" I asked sincerely concerned.

As Billy came closer to me, I could see his face riddled with tension. A furious looking frown adorned his face, and he was biting his lip.

I slowly stood up as fear gripped me. A large achy lump formed in my throat, as I tried to shake the fear that was racing through my body.

"Billy, I was concerned about you. Did you work late again? I --

Billy grabbed me by my arm and gave me the harshest look. He drew back his hand and came down across my face.

"Billy…. Stop…. Please…. I'm sorry," I pleaded.

"Damn right you are sorry. Always asking me where I've been…. Why I'm late. Who in the hell do you think you are to question me?" he snarled.

"No Billy…. Please don't --

Billy's hand came across my face hard again, this time knocking me to the floor.

I scrambled to get up and get away. Billy walked up to me quickly and bent down and lifted me partially off the floor with one hand and drew his fist with the other.

"Billy no-o-o-o-o-o! No-o-o-o-o-o!" I screamed.

Billy hit me three more times, with the final blow coming across my eye. The intense pain riveted through my head, leaving me writhing on the floor.

"Never ever ask me where I've been," Billy shouted as he turned and stomped back out of the house, slamming the door behind him.

I lay there on the floor for what seemed like hours. I finally summoned enough strength to pull myself up from the floor. I staggered to the bathroom to try to wash my face. When I looked into the mirror, one of my eyes was nearly swollen shut, and blood was seeping from my nose. I looked horrible and my head hurt badly. I managed to stop my nose from bleeding and went to the fridge to get ice to make a cold compress for my eye.

I took some aspirin and got my cold compress and went to the bedroom. I crawled into bed and held the compress to my swollen eye. As I lay there, tears slid down my face. Why did Billy do this to me? He literally beat me -- and with no remorse. He abused me and just left, not even giving what he did a second thought.

The reality of Sam's words now ripped at my heart. How much of Billy's abuse would it take before I accept that he is abusive, selfish and manipulative?

I felt so alone and abandoned. That night, I cried until I fell asleep -- hurt, overwhelmed, and broken-hearted.

Chapter

THIRTEEN

Over the next few months, Billy changed drastically. He came home late into the night frequently and he always seemed to have some important out-of-town meeting that was urgent and needed his immediate attention. I was just over four months along now and Billy rarely asked how I was or showed very much concern about our baby or me.

Billy continually did an excellent job for his clients, making sure that their wishes became reality. I was proud that he was so dedicated to them, but I was becoming so lonely. I also was a bit jealous because they seemed to get more of his time than I did now.

Billy became more and more distant and never spent much time with me anymore. He would sometimes give me a quick kiss in the mornings before he left, and it would be very late when he returned. I often fell asleep trying to wait up for him. He definitely was losing interest in our baby and me because he hardly ever asked about my check-ups and had not showed any enthusiasm about my pregnancy in many months.

* * * * * * *

Upon awaking this morning, I felt so alone and Billy had already gone to work. In an attempt to overcome the lonely, hollow feeling I had so often, I dressed and went for a walk in the park. I had become a regular to this park over the past few months it seemed to have calming, tranquil qualities. The long walks helped to cleanse my spirits and mind, and walking also was good exercise for me.

Sometimes though while on my walks, I would run into couples happily eating together or they would just be lovingly holding hands as they walked. This would bring back memories of when Billy and I shared precious times together. Remembering when we first married, we were so much in love, just as the couples I saw at the park were. There were so many things that we used to do together, just as these couples do. Now I drift off to sleep alone in our bed mostly every night.

The next afternoon, I went on another walk in the park. I became tired, so I decided to rest for a while on one of the benches. I admired a couple embrace and exchange a loving kiss. The tenderness and the love that they were sharing brought tears to my eyes, as I remembered my longing for Billy's affection…. How I ached for him to hold me the way he used to and love me tenderly.

"A penny for your thoughts," a strange voice said, interrupting my train of thought.

Startled, I turned around and looked into the warmest, most caring, soft, brown eyes.

"Hi…. Lynnette…. Do you remember me? You went to Whitmore High didn't you?" he asked solemnly.

"Uh –h –h yes…. Of course I did," I stammered

"I was the guy most of the kids in school had called *Steve the Nerd*," he spoke softly. "I'm Steve Montgomery. My family and I moved away when I was still in high school …. well I think it was junior high school."

"Why sure…. I remember you now. Most of the kids did tease you in school. I tried to defend you back then because I tried to tell the kids that that was very mean and that you were really a very sweet guy if they had tried to get to know you."

"I know Lynnette…. I remember."

"You know Steve, you were very smart," I pointed out.

"I always had thought of you as a bookworm and you were so shy," I said, closely observing his face and physique.

It had been seven years since I'd seen Steve. We had studied together occasionally in school and I guess you could say that we were sort of like friends. But this man standing before me now was so handsome and refined. His physical features had changed drastically over the past seven years. He no longer was the drab-looking, clumsy kid I remembered from back in school.

As a tear slid down my face, I looked at him and I could see genuine concern in his face.

"Lynnette…. My goodness…. Whatever your problem might be, it will get better. Nothing can be that bad."

If only he knew the trials I have been through over the past months I thought. Steve had always been a sweet, compassionate person, even when we were in school. He was just that type of person that you could confide in and I liked him for it.

"Lynnette…. I have been noticing you coming out here for a month now. I had been trying to figure out how to approach you," Steve says, as he politely joins me on the bench.

"This park is so beautiful that I spend as much time as I can out here. I come out here to think and it also helps me to clear my head," he added.

"Oh, yes…. Me too. I love this park," I said, trying to muster a smile. "I've had so many things on my mind these past months. I come out here to try to sort them through."

"How has life really been for you, Steve?"

"Well…. I've been here in Charleston for about a year trying to get settled into my law practice. One day, I drove past this park on my way home and noticed how beautiful it was, and I have been coming out here ever since. That's around the time I first saw you here."

"Lynnette…. You know, you're still just as lovely as I remember. I wanted to reach out to you, but some of my old shyness made me be a coward. I also didn't want to intrude because you seemed to be so heavy in thought…. Didn't want to invade your space. I wouldn't have approached you today, but you seemed more troubled than I had seen you before and I felt that just maybe I could offer you my help if you wanted or needed it. So tell me…. why are you so upset Lynnette?" he asked sympathetically, looking deep into my eyes.

I did need someone to talk to because my heart was so burdened with despair. After seeing the concern and care in Steve's eyes, I confided in him. He had always been very easy to talk to in the past.

"Steve…. I married Billy Matthews. Do you remember him from our school?" I asked.

"Yeah…. He was the football jock right…. a lot of girls had a crush on him. I can remember that all through high school I had secretly wished that I was that popular, because none of the girls noticed me except when they were laughing or making fun at me." He spoke soberly, as if that thought still pained his mind.

"Well…. up until a few months ago, Billy and I were as happy as could be. He is doing well in his job and we're expecting our first child. Sometime after that, Billy began changing."

"Changing in what way?" Steve questioned.

"He would come home very late at night…. He's hit me a few times…. And…. Steve…. He…. He's using drugs."

I began sobbing uncontrollably, as the tears flowed down my face. I turned from Steve because I was so ashamed and I really didn't want him to see me this way. My throat ached, as I tried desperately to choke back the overwhelming sadness I felt.

Steve came around in front of me and cradled my trembling hands in his, as he tried to comfort me.

"Lynnie…. Please…. Don't cry. I realize that this is an awful lot for you to contend with, but you know what? I will be there for you, anytime that you need me," Steve said softly, lifting my tear soaked face.

Steve pulled me into his arms, and I felt security that I had not experienced for a long time. He stroked my weary head, as I clung to him as if he were my lifeline.

Abruptly, I pulled away, as I realized suddenly that we were so intimate. I could feel the blood rushing to my cheeks.

"I…. I…. I'm sorry Steve. I…. I really didn't mean to just hang all over you like that," I stammered apologetically.

"Hey…. It's okay Lynnie…. I didn't mind it at all. You needed to get that crying out of system. These shoulders are here for you to cry on anytime you need them," Steve said, steering my head toward him. "You will always have me as your friend."

A single tear drifted aimlessly from my eye, as I looked into Steve's soothing, gentle eyes. He looked at me and smiled, as he brushed the tear away.

"Now Lynnie, tell me…. That is, if it's comfortable for you to talk about it…. What else has Billy done?"

"Well…. I'm alone most of the time. Billy hardly spends time with me like he used to do. I know that he has to work, but he used to make time for me. I miss that Steve."

Steve and I began walking, as I swallowed hard to push down the lump in my throat so that I could continue. Steve listened attentively.

"When Billy's not out of town on business meetings, he's coming home late at night. I'm realistic enough to know that he has to keep odd hours sometimes, but he's almost totally neglecting me, and it hurts terribly. When he gets up in the morning, I try to catch him before he leaves so that we can talk. Some mornings, he leaves so quietly that I don't even awake until long after he's gone. Whenever he is at home, he's rushing around so fast that I don't get to say much. He would give me a quick peck on the cheek and then rush out the door.

I stopped walking momentarily, turning to face Steve. He reached out and gathered both my hands in his, as I looked at him through misty eyes.

"Steve…. I just don't know what to do anymore," I blubbered, as the tears showered my face.

I dropped my head because I was so ashamed to look into Steve's face.

Steve reached out and raised my tear-drenched face and used his handkerchief to softly wipe tears away.

"Oh Lynnie…. I hate to see you hurting this way so badly," Steve said, sympathetically.

When Steve felt that I was calmer, he walked me home and made me promise that I would stay in touch. He smiled a crooked grin at me, as he disappeared around the corner.

Chapter

FOURTEEN

When I awoke this morning, I was in much better spirits. I guess the talk that I'd had with Steve had helped a lot. It felt good having a friend from my past so near me that I could talk with whenever I needed. Our friendship goes back almost as far as Billy and I do, and Steve really listens to me…. he always did. Sam and Dee had stopped visiting so often, since Billy acted so badly toward them. I saw them occasionally; maybe several times a month, and then we only engaged in short, general conversation. Billy had caused me to become alienated from the friends I had, until I saw Steve at the park.

The day seemed to rush by, as I went about doing my daily chores. I had gotten Billy's dinner underway, but I felt a little tired. As I sat down and reclined on the sofa, I let out a long sigh of relief. I began getting drowsy, so I just stretched out and dozed soundly asleep.

I was awakened abruptly by the front door slamming shut. As I sat up on the sofa, I heard Billy's voice rang out.

"Lynnie! What's this I hear about some guy leaving my house?" He snapped.

"B…. Billy…. Why are you yelling at me?" I asked innocently.

"Don't try to play that naïve game on me," he yelled. "You know what I'm talking about. Are you sneaking around with this guy?" He asked accusingly.

"Billy…. Please…. You are all wrong about this," I pleaded. "Steve is just a friend from our school back home. I hadn't seen or heard from him since we were all in school back then and I didn't learn until just today that he was here."

"Don't lie to me Lynnie, damn it…. Don't lie to me!"

"But I'm not lying Billy…. This is the truth…. I wouldn't lie to you… I love you…. Don't you realize that by now? I ran into Steve when I went for a walk at the park and he just walked me home. Nothing happened honey…. There is nothing going on…. You've got to believe me," I begged.

"You're a damn liar," Billy snarled.

Billy looked at me with such contempt that it seemed to penetrate straight through me. This was the absolute worst that I had ever seen Billy. I stared at him wide-eyed, as my body quaked with fear, awaiting his next cruel, accusing remark.

"Lynnie…. That damn baby that you are carrying…. It's probably his isn't it? Well don't expect me to take care of another man's bastard child. As far as I know, you could have been seeing him for months while I was away on business trips. Let your precious Steve take care of your baby," Billy yelled angrily.

I grabbed his hand in a desperate attempt to get him to listen to me.

"Billy…. You…. You don't understand…. Please Billy…. You've got it all wrong…. really…. I had not seen Steve until today," I said, sobbing mercifully. "I love you and there's been no one else."

Billy jerked away from me and gave me the most dreadful look that jabbed through my heart like a knife.

"You can have an abortion for all I care because I'm not having a damn thing to do with that baby," Billy growled. "You're nothing but a fucking bitch!"

Suddenly, Billy drew his hand up and came across my face, knocking me on the sofa.

"You and Steve can go to hell, because I don't give a damn! I'm done with you Lynn!"

Billy turned and stormed out the door, leaving me lying there mortified and hurt. I lay there on the sofa, drowning in my own tears. All the hurtful things that Billy had said kept replaying in my head. Nothing was making any sense at this point because Billy had no foundation for his accusations. I have always been true to him and had given him no reason at all to worry or doubt me. He was my life and was all that I needed and I had built my total existence around him. Sure, Billy had his faults as anyone else would, but none of that mattered to me. I loved him and all of his faults because I believe that when you really love someone, you accept their weaknesses and faults alike. Over the past months, Billy had become chauvinistic and lived by a double standard. I still love him even though he has treated me rather badly.

I also reflected on how devoted I had been to Billy because I had almost severed all ties with my friends because of his angry, resentful attitude toward them. I had abandoned my friends and went along with all of his selfish, self-centered desires. Now I guess he was going to leave me ….. Desert me …. Toss me to the side like I was nothing but trash.

I brushed my tears away and thought that maybe a hot bath would soothe some of the frustrations that seemed to torment me. Forcing myself up from the sofa, I went upstairs and ran a full bath and added my favorite scented oil. Slipping into the warm, soft water, I slowly slid down into the water until it reached my neck, allowing my head to rest on the bath pillow. Closing my eyes, I allowed my mind to drift aimlessly until I dozed off.

I awakened a short time later, as the water had cooled. I toweled off and threw on a large, comfortable caftan and lay across the bed. The bath did help to relax me and it had taken away much of the tension. I put on my pajamas and climbed into bed. I was feeling so alone. As I lay there clutching a pillow, I drifted off to sleep again, hoping that more of my pain and hurt would subside.

* * * * * * * *

The next morning I was scheduled for another check-up, so I dressed and went into town.

The scenery that I used to admire on the way into the city now went by in a blur of light and dark images. As I approached the exit, I managed to concentrate enough to make my exit on Washington Boulevard. After several blocks, I pulled into South Carolina Regional Medical Center.

Dr. Balthrop told me that my pregnancy was still coming along nicely. I was almost at my fifth month and displayed a small bulge. I was very pleased to know that everything was still fine because I didn't want anything to happen to my baby. I was advised to watch my diet carefully and tried to get plenty of rest.

On the way home, I stopped off at the store to pick up some things for supper. While I shopped, I thought of calling Billy to tell him that I wanted to try to resolve our differences from yesterday and that I was preparing a special meal for the two of us. I really wanted to work things out and was willing to forget the hurtful things he had said to me, if he would just tell me that he still loved me.

After paying the clerk at the counter, I gathered my two bags and walked back to my car. Just before I approached it, the bottom ripped out of my bag and canned goods rolled in all directions across the parking lot. I sighed, as I placed the other bag on the hood of my car and turned to begin picking up the stray cans.

"Let me get that for you Lynnie," a deep, concerned voice said.

Turning around to thank the nice gentleman who had come to my aid, I faced Steve standing there smiling broadly. What a welcome sight I thought, as I flashed him a pleasant smile.

"Thanks Steve for offering to help."

"I don't mind Lynnie. I'd do anything to keep that beautiful smile on your face…. and to help you in any way that I can. I'll have all of this up for you in a jiffy," he said, while gathering the cans in his muscular arms.

Steve stood to face me and his brow creased with concern.

"How have you been Lynnie since we last talked?"

Remembering the huge argument Billy and I had yesterday, sadness swept over me, but I didn't want to try to explain that to Steve right now. I looked up at Steve in a serious but humble way.

"Steve…. I do appreciate the kindness you have shown me. You are a good man."

Steve managed a slight smile, but he had a puzzled appearance on his face.

"It's Billy isn't it? You've told me about the way he has been acting. I know that you love him a great deal because if you didn't, you wouldn't have gone through all of this nonsense. Why in the hell can't the fool see what kind of woman he has in you?" Steve remarked, in an agitated tone.

Steve placed my groceries in the trunk of my car and closed it hard. He stood there for a moment as if he were trying to calm himself. Then he spoke in a calmer voice. "I apologize for speaking like that Lynnie. It just upsets me that he treats you this way.

Steve took out a note pad and scribbled on it.

"This is my number Lynnie. You call me day or night if you need anything, okay. I also want you to tell me what's really going on when you feel that you are ready to talk about it."

Steve opened the car door for me and I seated myself. I managed to muster up a fake smile for him, as he closed my door. But I was so preoccupied with the thought of Billy's harsh words that their effect still tugged at my heart.

Steve returned me a brilliant smile and waved good-bye.

After arriving home, I put away my groceries. Though I still wanted to phone Billy, the idea made me too nervous. A refreshing showered showed much more promise and was very appealing. So I went upstairs hoping that the shower could work its magic for me again, because I needed to shower away some of the frustrations that gripped my tense body.

After my shower I felt great. I was much more relaxed and felt good enough to start supper. The one thing about when I was preparing supper for Billy was that I never knew if he was going to come home or not.

I sat down at the kitchen table and my mind drifted off to thoughts of Billy and how he has changed. I also was feeling sorry for how pathetic I had become. I just seemed to keep doing the wrong thing in Billy's eyes.

Over the past months Billy had gone through a metamorphosis. His attitude and personality had taken on this Jekyll and Hyde persona. I never knew from one time to another if what I was doing or saying was going to be right to him. It seemed that I could never do anything right. Billy was making me start to feel insecure…. and I believed him when he said that no one else would want a woman like me…. one so helpless and incapable of doing anything right.

Billy's violent behavior seemed to progress more with

time and each time he hurt me, he would apologize and promise not to do it again, but he did. It seemed as though just about anything would set him off and he would morph into this man I can barely recognize.

I was drawing farther and farther away from my friends Sam and Dee. I felt ashamed.... ashamed of how worthless I was.... that I was failing, because I could not run a home right and could not give Billy the happiness that he was due. After all, wasn't Billy supporting me?

I was become afraid of Billy.... afraid of what he would do to me if I told half of the things he had done to me. He had also warned me of the consequences if I ever told.... and I believed that he would do just as he said.

Marriage, I thought to myself, shouldn't have to be like this.... the violence.... the unspeakable vile words and anger. But what could I do. I love Billy still even though he treated me this way. I just didn't want to give up on him.... I just didn't want give up.

After some thought, I decided to go ahead and fix supper. I still wasn't certain that Billy would show. But if he came home and supper wasn't ready, it would set him off. I felt like I was, as the saying goes, *"between a rock and a hard place."*

After I had gotten supper ready, I fixed myself a plate and went into the living room. I wanted to watch T.V. in the living room for a change. I wanted to see Star Trek since I was a *"trekkie,"* a term that we used to describe die-hard Star Trek fans.

After a few hours of T.V., I collected my plate and went back to the kitchen to clean up things. Glancing up at the clock on the wall, I saw that it was almost 10 p.m. I was pretty sure now that this would be one of those nights that Billy wouldn't be home. I had really wanted to talk to him about the misunderstanding we had about Steve, but as usual, my desire and need to communicate with my husband was a bust.

Later that night when I went to bed, I felt so alone, as I looked sadly over my shoulder at the pillow where Billy used to lay his head every night.

You should be use to these lonely nights Lynnie, I thought to myself. *This isn't the first time that Billy has not come home.*

A stray tear coursed down my cheek, as I turned over and hugged Billy's pillow tightly. I longed for him to be here with me, but once again, I fell asleep hurt, sad, and alone.

* * * * * * *

When I awakened this morning, my spirits were somewhat low. Somehow, I managed to get up and out of bed and start my day. Since I was being health-conscious about my diet during my pregnancy, I made a healthy breakfast, which consisted of low-fat yogurt, a slice of bacon, a small bagel with jelly, a banana and a glass of milk.

After breakfast, I dressed and went for a short walk in the park. The day was so sunny and bright. The fresh air and the walk would be good for me and it helped to clear my head.

After my walk in the park, I headed for the mall. I really enjoyed browsing the baby sections in the stores. Of course…. you know that I couldn't resist buying a few items.

When I was done with all of my browsing, I went into this store called O'Charley's. I absolutely love their homemade yeast rolls and their signature caramel pies, so I picked up some of each to take home.

On the way home, thoughts of Billy crept back into my mind. He didn't come home last night nor did he come in this morning to get a change of clothes. I wondered where he was and if he was okay.

When I arrived home, I gathered my shopping bags together to carry inside. When I approached the door, I noticed that it was ajar and I knew that I didn't leave it open when I left this morning. I sit my bags down and swallowed hard. A sudden sharp twinge coursed through my body, as I slowly pushed the door fully open. After summoning the courage to go inside, I stepped into the house. Looking about the room, it appeared to have been ransacked…. lamps were knocked over…. pillow cushions had been thrown about and ripped open….

pictures were broken…. The room was a sight…. a real mess.

Instinctively, I quickly stepped back outside and called Sam on my cell phone. She told me to just sit tight, that she would be here shortly.

Sam had Dee with her when she pulled into the driveway. I explained to them what I had found when I got home and that I went no farther than the living room.

Sam, Dee and I went inside together and searched every room of the house. We didn't see anyone in the house, but found more things broken and thrown around. In the bedroom, we all walked around the pillage on the floor. This room apparently had more destruction done to it. Sam suggested that we call the police.

Looking over at the walk-in closet, I noticed clothes and hangers lying partially out of the door. I slowly made my way to the closet door, and opened it. One whole side of the closet was empty. My heart was starting to race now, as a horrible thought consumed me.

"What's wrong Lynnie…. girl you look like you've seen a ghost," Sam remarked.

I rushed to Billy's dresser and began opening drawers. Each drawer that I opened was empty. An ach lump formed in my throat, as I began mumbling incoherently.

"He can't be…. he can't be…. left me…. he can't be," I mumbled.

Suddenly feeling weak in the knees, I eased over to the bed and plopped down.

"What are you talking about Lynnie? What's wrong?" Sam asked with concern in her voice.

"Yeah…. Lynnie…. you don't look so good," Dee added.

Suddenly, at that very moment it hit me. "I know what had happened here," I said, in a strained voice.

"What are you taking about…? What do you mean you know what happened? Sam asked in a raised voice.

"We won't have to call the police…. Billy has left me," I said, dropping my head.

I paused for moment, gathering strength to continue.

"All of Billy's clothes are gone…. all of his clothes from the closet as well as the clothes in the dresser. I guess he was so angry when he came home that he just tore up and broke things everywhere.

Looking into Sam's face I could see that she was enraged at Billy's actions.

"Your husband is a crazy son of a bitch. He wasn't even man enough to face you. So I guess he waited until you left and did all this shit. He's nothing but a damn two-bit coward…. I've always believed that about him. I say good riddance to his sorry ass."

Looking up at Sam with tears streaming down my face, I was utterly distraught and overwhelmed. Seeing me this way Sam clamed down, and sit near me on the bed, taking my hands in hers.

"Look Lynnie…. I apologize for getting so upset because you really don't need my actions to deal with along with what you already have to deal with now. But the content of what I said is true. You may not be able to see this now, but you will be better off without Billy in your life. He has no respect for you or your baby…. hell…. he don't even have respect for himself. Lynnie…. just know that you are not alone girl. Dee and I will always be here whenever you may need us. Right Dee?'

"Oh absolutely…. we'll always be your friend Lynnie," Dee added.

The three of us sat there on the bed with our arms around each other. Though I had lost the love of my life, I was very happy to have such great friends.

Dee and Sam helped me straighten up the house. It took us nearly the rest of the day to get things back in order, but we did it.

After all that hard work, we made sandwiches and had a salad. I showed Dee and Sam the things I had gotten for the baby today when I went to the mall. My friends and I just sat and enjoyed chatting with each other for a while…. which was something I had missed doing with them for such a long time.

Sam and Dee had to get home. Greg was taking Dee to a musical stage play and had invited Sam to come along. They invited me to go too, but I really didn't feel up it. Sam and Dee told me that they would check back on me later, said their good-byes and left for home.

After Sam and Dee left, the house was so quite. Making up my mind to get supper started, I went into the kitchen and chose a nice cut of sirloin that I had purchased yesterday. I prepared the steak with rosemary sauce and served it with broccoli and cheese, a baked potato, and a salad.

Suddenly my mind veered back to Billy, as I was placing the silverware on the table. Overwhelmed with thoughts of my husband, I dropped down in one of the chairs at the kitchen table. Then all of a sudden, I remembered Steve giving me his number. I could really use a friendly ear I thought. I retrieved the phone number and called upon Steve. And true to his word, he told me that he would be right there. After hanging up the phone, overpowering grief engulfed me, as tears welled in my eyes. My sadness was so intense that I just couldn't contain it any longer and I began sobbing. Cradling my head in my hands, the tears flowed freely.

Why did you do this to me Billy, I told myself. *Why have you hurt me so badly? I didn't do anything to deserve this sort of ill treatment.*

My sobbing was interrupted when someone rang the doorbell. I wiped away my tears and dragged myself to the door. When I opened it, there stood Steve.

"Lynnie.... My goodness.... What's wrong?" he exclaimed. "Billy has done something.... I just know it. If he hit you, I'll put my foot in his--

"Billy didn't hit me," I interrupted. "He's left me Steve.... Billy has packed up all of his things and left me," I burbled out. "He left no note or anything. I don't understand Steve.... I really don't understand.... What did I do?"

Steve stepped inside and closed the door behind him. He had the most concerned, caring look on his face. When he extended his arms to me, I slowly eased into them. Steve held me in such a gentle, firm way that I totally succumbed to his comforting touch. I was so relieved to have someone hold me and gently soothe away the pain that I allowed my tears to flow freely.... as freely as an April shower.

Steve held me tightly and told me that he would be there to help me get through this ordeal. Deep down, I felt that he would really be there for me through this trying time in my life.

Chapter

FIFTEEN

After Billy's departure, I had to fight constantly to keep depression from overcoming me. The coming months would prove to be tedious and would really test my faith. I thanked God for having the good sense to put back some money for a rainy day. My Mom and Dad had instilled self-reliance into me at an early age. My parents tried to convince me to come home. Since I was determined to stay, they sent me money to help me out whenever I needed it or not during this trying time. I was also so thankful for having great friends like Sam, Dee, and Steve. They all joined forces to ensure that I kept my sanity and they kept my mind stimulated with constructive and fun things to do. My friends were there for me.... they listened and let me talk about my feelings.... They believed all of my stories about how Billy treated me.... they never judged me.... and they didn't criticize me for staying with him as long as I did. Most of all, they assured me that I was not to blame for Billy's behavior. My friends supported and encouraged me so that I would be capable of making the right choices for me.

Today was December 14th, and it was only twelve days from Christmas. If Billy and I had stayed together, it would have been our second Christmas together.

Getting out of bed this morning was a chore. I had not slept very much and my baby has been kicking up a storm. I had made a pot of coffee and had just finished trying to eat my breakfast. I did manage to eat a piece of toast and was just sitting at the kitchen table sipping on a cup of coffee.

I got up from the table and walked over to the patio door and opened the vertical blinds. I stood there fro a while drinking my coffee and watching the leaves swirl around in the backyard. I had hung a bird feeder in the big magnolia tree. There were several blue jays eating the seed mix I had put there when it first turned cold. The brisk wind swayed the swing that sits on the patio that Billy and I had assembled together.

The ringing phone broke my melancholy mood.

"Good morning gorgeous," a deep voice echoed

through the line.

"How is my girl today?"

"Hi Steve…. I…. I'm okay," I said lowly.

"You really don't sound okay to me," Steve said with concern in his voice.

"We are going to have to work on your enthusiasm young lady. This moping about will never do. Ummmm…. let's see. How about I pick you up and take you out to lunch?"

"Uhhhhh I don't know Steve."

"Well…. I'm not taking no for an answer…. so what do you say?"

"Oh alright…. I'll go to lunch with you."

"Great…. I'll be there to pick you up…. say around 11:30?"

"Sure…. I'll be ready Steve," I said, smiling to myself.

After Steve had hung up, I reflected on how attentive he has been throughout my ordeal. Steve tries his best to keep me occupied so that I don't have time to dwell on being lonely and hurt. Steve is the total opposite of Billy. He listens to me…. he really listens. He doesn't treat me like I am a screw-up. He is compassionate, caring, funny, sensitive…. and let's not forget…. handsome as hell.

"Whew…. I can't believe that I'm thinking this way about Steve. But he is so easy and comfortable to be with and I enjoy his company. Billy has been gone for several months now and I should try to go on without him. I need to accept the fact that Billy's love for me changed and I had to stop blaming myself for all of our problems. I am so grateful to have friends who care enough to not allow me to wallow in self-pity and sink into depression.

I did a few small chores around the house, and then got ready for my lunch date with Steve. I was actually looking forward to lunch with Steve.

Steve arrived right on schedule and I was dressed and ready to go.

Sermet's Corner was Steve's place of choice for lunch. I really enjoyed eating there because of its large windows overlooking the bustling intersection and its fun atmosphere. Their cuisine was fresh, informal, and healthy. Sermet's Corner also had live jazz in the mezzanine Tuesday to Saturday. Steve promised to bring me back so that I can experience this exceptional treat.

Steve and I had a very enjoyable, long lunch. He wanted to know about any dreams or aspirations that I might have…. long term or short term. He encouraged me to speak freely and told me that I should follow my dreams.

Steve and I had really enjoyed our conversation up until a soberly, dreamy look came over his handsome face. That expression on his face concerned me and I wanted to reach out to him.

"Is something wrong Steve?" I asked in a sincere voice.

Steve's dark eyes captured mine, as his facial expression turned serious. After a little hesitation, he spoke.

"Actually Lynnie…. there is something wrong."

Steve gathered my hands into his, as he seemed to be in a serious battle with his conscious.

"Lynnie…. I need to confess something to you. I have held this inside for so long and I just can't do it anymore."

My heart was racing now because I wasn't sure of what Steve was about to tell me. I knew that my attraction to him had grown over these past months, but I had been too afraid to speak about those feelings. I didn't think I was supposed to feel those kinds of feelings for anyone except Billy. Now I have budding feelings for Steve and secretly hoped that he has these feelings too.

"Go ahead Steve…. tell me what's on your mind," I encouraged.

"Okay…. here it is. I have had feelings for you and have cared about you since we were in school, but I could never tell you. You had a boyfriend and…. Well…. I was *the nerd*. It was easier just being a friend to you than admitting my true feelings. Now that I have found you again and…. Well…. Since Billy is gone, I told myself that I was given a second chance to be honest about my feelings for you. Honestly Lynnie…. I have been in love with you since high school. I love you Lynnie…. I always have and always will."

My face felt flushed, as I looked into Steve's gentle, solemn face. I knew then that his feelings were genuine.

"Steve…. I…. I don't know what to say," I stuttered, searching for the right words to say.

"Steve…. I…"

Steve interrupted me in mid sentence.

"I'm not going to push you, okay? We can proceed at your own pace. I just wanted you to know how I felt. I want to be with you and I want you to be a part of my life.

Steve's acknowledgement of his true feelings was music to my ears and affirmed what I had been sensing…. These were the words I had secretly hoped he would say. I was so moved by Steve's confession that I gently and lovingly touched his solemn face.

"Steve…. my feelings for you have been growing stronger for months now and I really appreciate your honesty with me.

I grasped Steve's hands in mine, as I looked into his deep, dark eyes.

"You are truly an exceptional man in every way. I will need for you to continue to patient with me a little longer. It has meant so much to me that you have not been putting pressure on me. I would like a chance to see where our relationship goes too. All I ask is that you bear with me a little longer. Can you give me this time…. will you give me this time Steve?"

"Of course…. yes…. yes…. anything you want sweetheart. We will just go one day at a time, okay?"

Steve took me home after our long lunch and he went back to work. As I sat and watched T.V., all I could think about was the things he had said to me. Steve's words just kept replaying in my mind. I kept trying to imagine a life with him…. Wondered what kind of father figure he would be for my baby.

* * * * * * *

As time went on, Steve and I kept getting closer and started spending more and more time together…. quality time…. whereas I had a chance to get to know him and for him to get to know me. Steve has been a godsend.

Today was Christmas Eve, and Steve and I had made plans of spending it with me. He had suggested that it might be nice to make rum balls and other Christmas goodies together. I thought that the idea might be fun and would give us a chance to spend quality time together.

Steve and I had lots of fun in the kitchen. We made rum balls, cheese balls, and cookies.

Steve and I had finished our baking and we were cleaning up the kitchen when he got a mischievous notion on his mind. He put his finger in some powdered sugar that we had left over in a small bowl, and quickly wiped it on my nose.

"Oh…. Steve…. you little devil…. I'm going to get you for that," I playfully threatened.

I put powdered sugar on both my hands and started chasing after him --- and I caught him too, though I'm pretty sure that he allowed me to catch him…. he wanted me to catch him.

Steve stopped running from me and turned around to face me. When he did, I put a powdered hand on each side of his handsome face. He looked so adorable with the white sugar on his face and it made me laugh.

Steve was laughing too. Then quickly and without hesitation, Steve kissed me on the nose.

"Ummmm…. the powdered sugar that I put on your nose tastes so good," he said smiling broadly.

I gestured with my finger for Steve to come closer to me. When he had gotten close enough, I kissed him gently on one cheek and then the other.

"Ummmm…. the powdered sugar on your cheeks tastes just as good and just as sweet," I said with a playful wink.

Steve and I both seemed to be pulled toward each other as if by some invisible magnet. When our lips met, it was heavenly. Our kiss was so full of passion that it made my body tingle with unfounded delight. In his kiss I felt love, and longing and thankfulness. Our kiss lingered, as Steve pulled me in closer to him. I succumbed completely to the growing intensity that expressed itself in our kiss. After Steve stopped kissing me and pulled away, I was left breathless. My face was suffused with happiness as

I looked at Steve. I was starting to realize that what was happening to me was that I was beginning to fall for Steve. *Has love discovered me and have I discovered love*, I thought.

I don't think Steve picked up on what I was feeling and thinking at this very moment. He just continued to look at me lovingly.

Steve broke the magical spell when he stepped back.

"Come on dearest…. Let's finish cleaning the kitchen," he said with a big smile.

After putting the finishing touches on the kitchen, Steve said that he should be getting home.

I walked Steve to the door, as we held hands.

"I love you, my dearest," he whispered and kissed me with confidence and fervor, embracing me tightly. When Steve released me and stepped back, I was breathless.

"I will see you in the morning my dearest Lynnie…. I love you," he said huskily.

"See you in the morning Steve," I whispered back.

I stood in the doorway and watched him get into his car and drive away. After closing the door, I went back into the living room and turned off the light by the chair, on one side of the sofa and then the other.

After getting ready for bed, I turned off the lamp near the bed and then slipped in under the covers. As I lay there, my thoughts were with Steve. Tonight had been such a wonderful experience…. everything was wonderful…. his playfulness and his sensual kisses. The thought of Steve kissing me made me smile contently.

After a while, the quietness and thoughts of Steve lulled me to fall into a sound, dreamless sleep.

Chapter
SIXTEEN

Christmas morning had arrived and I woke up feeling great for the first time in a long time. I actually got a chance to sleep comfortably through the night.

I got up, got dressed, put on a pot of coffee, and made a light breakfast. I was looking forward to seeing Steve today.

As I sat sipping my coffee and eating on a bagel, the doorbell rang.

Of course it was Steve when I answered the door, standing there with a huge grin on his face and carrying an armful of gifts.

"Good morning my dearest…. Merry Christmas," he

said graciously.

"Come on in Steve," I said smiling and stepping aside so that he could come in.

Steve came in and placed the gifts on the sofa and turned around, pulled me into his arms, and kissed me gently.

"All of these gifts are for you sweetie. I wanted you to have a memorable Christmas. You deserve it," Steve boasted.

"Thank you for all of the gifts, but first I want you to come and eat breakfast with me, okay?"

"Okay…. And then you are opening all of your gifts, right?"

"Yes…. I promise," I said, grabbing him by the hand and taking him to the kitchen.

Steve and I enjoyed breakfast together and laughed and chatted for quite a while.

After breakfast Steve and I returned to the living room whereas he was anxious for me to start opening up the gifts he had gotten me.

One of the boxes contained a beautiful, ivory dress. The dress was made of silk with ivory lace overlay. Another box had yet another beautiful dress. It was a red, silk, strapless dress that had an unusual, raised brocade pattern.

Now what were left were two small boxes, one that was square-shaped and the other was rectangular. I chose to open the rectangular box first. I picked up the box and admired the beautiful wrapping and the curly bow on top. When I tore the wrapping paper from around the velvet box and opened it, it had a beautiful tennis bracelet inside. My eyes widened with amazement at the beauty of this bracelet, the diamonds and the intricate details of the design.

Finally, I picked up the last gift to open. This was the smaller square box and it really had peaked my interest. I looked over at Steve who was just sitting there smiling with happiness in his eyes.

"Go ahead sweetie…. open it…. it won't bite," Steve encouraged.

I pulled the wrapping from the box and opened it. Inside I found the most exquisite pair of diamond earrings.

I sat there admiring the earrings and all of the other marvelous gifts Steve had bought me. A single tear trailed down my face.

"Oh-h-h-h…. what's wrong sweetheart? Why the tears?" Steve asked, as he slid over next to me.

"I'm just so happy Steve…. I'm just happy."

Steve pulled me into his arms and held me close, laying his cheek against my hair. I felt so secure whenever Steve held me…. a security I had not felt in such a long time. It felt so good to be able to feel that safe and loved again. I wondered if I would get a chance to learn the full impact of Steve's love.

I carried my gifts to my bedroom, hanging my two dresses in the closet and placing the tennis bracelet and earrings in my jewelry box.

When I returned to the living room, Steve had put on a Blues and Soul Christmas album and Luther Vandross was singing "*A Kiss for Christmas.*"

"Come and dance with me dearest," Steve said, reaching for my hand.

As we danced, Steve held me close and we looked into each other's eyes.

"Steve…. I'd like to ask you something?"

"Sure sweetie…. what is it," he replied with a smile.

"Does it not bother you that I'm pregnant and that I'm as large as I am?" I asked innocently.

Steve stopped dancing, grabbed me by the hand, and led me over to the sofa to sit down. He gathered my hands into his and looked at me very seriously, but with his face still holding its solemn appeal.

"Look Lynnie…. sweetheart…. I want to be with you…. I love you. You could never be anything more than gorgeous in my eyes; I don't care what you do. You are as beautiful inside as you are outside. Even right now, to me you are even more beautiful because of your motherly glow. You could put on a flour sack and still be gorgeous to me."

I could feel the tears teasing the corners of my eyes and I started to lower my head. Steve quickly placed his gentle hand under my chin and lifted it back up until my eyes met his. He kissed me lightly at first, and then with more intensity and passion. Finally, Steve released me.

"I'm sorry, my dearest." He said. "I didn't mean to be so forward with you. You just intoxicate me so -- that I lose my head."

Steve looked at me, his eyes stormy, dark, and filled with emotion. I felt like I needed to come clean with Steve about how I really felt about him. I too, was feeling all sorts of sensations. I was feeling a whole range of feelings and sensations I had not experienced before, not even with Billy. Billy had awakened excitement in me, but with Steve it was different. I was beginning to see great depths of emotion in him and was finding a growing response in me. My body had started sending out all kinds of messages to me. I was falling for Steve, but was afraid to admit to him how I felt. Steve had started to feel like a part of me, so why was it so hard to admit my feelings for him.

Steve and I enjoyed the rest of the day and part of the night together until Steve announced that it was time for him to go. I resisted the melancholy feelings that I was experiencing because I didn't want Steve to see me upset. For some reason, I hated to see him go. I managed to maintain an upbeat appearance for Steve's sake.

As I walked Steve to the door, my eyes tried to become misty and a little sadness stirred deep within.

"I had a great time with you Lynnie," Steve spoke softly. "If you need anything…. anything at all…. please let me know, okay?"

"I will Steve…. I promise."

Steve kissed me gently and turned to leave. Suddenly, an overwhelming feeling rose quickly within me and I couldn't stifle this emotion this time.

"Steve…. wait…. don't go yet…. I need to tell you something," I blurted out nervously.

It was now or never, I silently confessed. *Tell the man how you really feel about him*, my inner voice said.

Steve turned around and stepped back into the house, but he displayed a puzzled appearance.

"What's wrong sweetie," he asked, following me back to the sofa.

I moved over closer to Steve on the sofa and grasped both his hands in mine. When I looked into his loving eyes, I knew that this was right. I placed one of my hands on his dear face and said, "I'm falling in love you Steve. My feelings are so overwhelming at times that I don't know what to do with it."

Steve's face began to change. First there was an incredulous expression that came over it. Then a look of blazing happiness came into his face and eyes.

"You must know, Lynnie, how long I've waited to hear you say those words," he whispered.

"I'm sorry that it took me so long, darling," I said softly.

Steve gathered me up in his arms and kissed me passionately. His kiss was so intoxicating that it took my breath away. When I pulled away, breathless, he loosened his embrace.

"I'm sorry dearest, I got carried away," he murmured into my hair.

"Steve," I whispered.

"Yes," he said, looking at my face as if he'd never seen it before.

"Do you believe that I'm falling in love with you?" I asked.

"Yes, my heart, I believe you," Steve said softly. "I don't know how I got so lucky, but I have to believe you love me as I love you or life won't make sense anymore."

I was so moved to give him reassurance that I kissed him. This time I felt a growing intensity *expressing* itself in my kiss. I sustained it as long as I could, and then pulled myself away. My heart was beating so wildly, that I put my hand to the spot and rubbed it for relief. Steve was breathing hard, his eyes dark with emotion.

We sat, eyes on each other, touching each other, basking in our newfound love.

"What now," I whispered.

"I think I'd better go before I will not want to," Steve admitted.

"I know.... I know.... You're right as usual," I replied soberly.

Steve and I moved slowly to the front door, arms around each other. At the door, we stood looking at each other and holding hands.

"I'm so happy, Steve," I said softly. "I can't believe this is true."

"I know, I feel the same way," Steve said.

I put my hand caressingly on his cheek. "Oh, Steve," I whispered.

Steve's eyes held hers with a fervent look. "Say the words to me again, Lynnie. I've waited so long to hear them," he whispered.

I said the words, softly, tenderly, making of them not only a declaration but also a commitment…. a promise.

I could sense that Steve didn't want to trust himself to embrace me, but he raised my lips to his and kissed me. In his kiss I felt love, longing, and passion.

Bless you, darling," he said. "Sleep well and dream of me," he said, managing a small smile.

Steve took the few steps to the door and turned the knob.

"Steve," I said in a small voice.

He turned back. I stood looking sad and bereft. In a second he stood before me.

"What is it, dearest?"

"You didn't want to hold me before you leave?" I asked simply, looking at him.

Steve made no answer in words. He put his arms around me and held me against him fitting my body to his. All of the other times at this door he'd offered her an embrace of rest and comfort. But tonight was a different matter. His beloved had acknowledged that she returned his love, and he was overwhelmed with intense emotions in which rest and comfort played no part.

Steve's embraces had always given me a sense of security and peace. Now, of course, I knew there was a difference in them because Steve and I were in love with each other. I wanted to learn the full impact of this difference. So I stood in his arms feeling safe and loved and wondering why I had to remind him of holding me.

As if I had spoken the words out loud, Steve whispered, "I didn't forget to hold you again, sweetheart. And it wasn't that I didn't want to. It was because I felt that I wouldn't want to let you go."

He tipped my head back and kissed me long and hard.

"Do you understand me, Lynnie," he whispered.

My eyes remained closed as I breathed, "Yes."

"Open your eyes, beloved," he whispered.

When I opened my eyes and he looked into them, he knew that I understood.

Steve kissed me again, tenderly. "Good night, my darling. I'll see you soon."

Chapter
SEVENTEEN

Four Months Later

Throughout the past months since Billy's departure, Steve came by the house everyday to check on me and to offer his assistance or his shoulder to cry on if I needed it. I would get a bit depressed sometime, but Steve wouldn't allow me to go into seclusion. I was in my eighth month of pregnancy and could barely see my feet. But my increasing size never bothered Steve. I felt that my being pregnant would make him turn away from me, but Steve didn't mind at all.

Steve had brought over some videos when he came to see me this evening. He had a miniature library that contained an assortment of comedy movies. He was extremely considerate -- always thinking of someone else when he or she is hurt and sad. Right now, he was my Good Samaritan.

"I have something here…. Something Ms. Lynnie that I'll guarantee will put a smile in that beautiful face. Step right over and have a seat," he said, with a playful wink.

"I'll go and pop some popcorn for us Steve and you can pick out a movie for us to watch. I shall return."

As Steve sorted through the movies, I glanced back over my shoulder and smiled at him on my way to the kitchen.

When I returned with the popcorn, I sat beside Steve and began looking through some of the movies. A particular video grabbed my attention. On the end of that video was the title, *"Forever Yours."* The title struck a cord deep within me, as tears began to tease the corners of my eyes. That movie title brought back many memories for me. I remembered how happy Billy and I had been earlier in our marriage…. I remembered the way that things used to be…. The love we had shared…. The baby we had created together. All of the bittersweet memories of our time together flooded the gate of my mind.

Tears began to slide down my face. Steve notices and sits the large bowl of popcorn on the table and slides over closer to me.

"Oh Lynnie…. honey…. Please…. Don't cry. What happened to bring all of this on?" he asked sincerely.

"It's silly…. Really. I was…. I was just looking through the videos…. And I…. I ran across this one and it sort of reminded me of my failed marriage. All of these…. These memories came rushing back and I just…. Just….

"Shhhhh, that's okay. I understand, but it will all pass honey. I will be here to help you through it. Don't be so hard on yourself. You 're doing great," Steve spoke optimistically.

For the first time since Steve had been here, I felt really comfortable with him. He knew just the right things to say to lift my spirits and I could sense the sincerity of his emotions. Steve was a good man and I wondered why someone hadn't snatched him up. He would have been a wonderful catch because of his compassionate, loving heart.

My train of thought was interrupted when Steve spoke.

"Are you okay now Lynnie?"

"Yes…. Sure…. Thank you Steve. I really don't know how I would have made it this far without you. You are a wonderful man," I said, with much admiration and respect.

"All right…. All right already. Enough with the compliments okay. You're going to embarrass me Lynnie," Steve said, lowering his head and displaying a hint of shyness.

I gently lifted his head with my hand and looked into his deep, dark eyes.

"I'm glad you are my friend Steve."

Steve grinned widely and we hugged again to seal our new level of friendship.

* * * * * * *

With Steve's help, I finally began allowing myself to heal from Billy's desertion, and the pain numbed as well. Steve wouldn't let me give up on life and living, though in the beginning I really felt like it. He was teaching me that just because things don't work out the way you want them the first time, doesn't mean that your life is over. He told me that I would fall in love again and that I shouldn't bury myself in grief forever. Steve had been wonderful and I admired his quiet strength. He helped me to attain the strength that I needed to repair my shattered life. He reminded me of how my child would need and depend on me when it arrived.

Steve and I grew closer and closer and it didn't matter to him if I was as big as the Goodyear blimp. I looked forward to seeing him and spending time with him. I no longer worried about Billy, or wondered why he never tried to contact me during the months he had been gone. He was now nothing more than a memory of my distant past, and I was working toward building a new life for my child and me. I secretly hoped that Steve would be a part of that life, but I was so afraid that he wouldn't feel the same as I did. I know that he cares for me and says that he loves me, but could he really, truly love me.

Steve took me out to dinner at a small, quaint, little restaurant called La Fontana. It was an Italian place that had a romantic aura about it because of its candlelit tables and soft music.

Steve selected a table that was secluded from the others. Just the thought of him being romantic made me tingly inside. All through dinner we laughed and enjoyed each other. Occasionally, we held hands and looked at each other lovingly. It was the perfect date…. every tantalizing, luscious moment of it.

On the way home, I snuggled up next to Steve and he draped his muscular arms over my shoulders. The closeness that Steve and I shared seemed so natural and we were so comfortable with each other. It was as if we had some type of invisible bond between us.

I invited Steve in after getting home and he agreed to stay for a while. The Grecian rain lamp in the corner of the living room gave the room a mysterious appearance as we entered it. The ample light that it cast was dim, but adequately lit the spacious room and gave it a romantic, sensual appeal.

I seated myself on the sofa, kicked off my shoes, and reclined back to allow my head to rest on its soft pillow.

Steve went to the stereo to find some music. He found a station that was playing song dedications. The station allowed people to call in and make special dedications to whomever they wished.

Suddenly, I sat upright on the sofa when I heard this announcement; "This song goes out to Lynnie Matthews from Steve Montgomery, with all his love."

Steve turned to me and slowly walked toward me with an extended hand.

"May I have this dance, Lynnie Matthews?"

The music began playing and I remembered the tune. The song was *Endless Love*.

Tears stung my eyes and a huge lump was forming in my throat. I looked deeply into Steve's eyes and I could clearly see the love that he felt for me. All of the doubts that I'd had about whether or not he loved me disappeared.

"I.... I'd love to Steve," I choked out, smiling ecstatically. "I'd love to."

Gently, Steve pulled me to my feet and into his awaiting arms. We spun around the floor several times with our eyes locked in a sensual gaze. Gradually, our dancing slowed to a standstill, as we seemed to be drawn to each other as if some unseen force was a pulling the two of us together. Steve stared deeply into my eyes as if trying to touch my soul and see my innermost thoughts. I was hopelessly under his spell and I did not waiver to any of his advances.

"You are so beautiful Lynnie," Steve said, stroking my face.

"I've fallen so deeply in love with you and want to spend the rest of my life making you and your baby happy. I'd like to help you raise your child and I will care and love it as if it were my own. Just say that you will be my wife Lynnie…. Will you marry me?"

Now, instead of tears of sorry and pain, flowed tears of joy and happiness. I was overwhelmed with the fact that Steve could love me so even though I gotten so large from my pregnancy was just so unbelievable to me. None of this seemed to matter to him. Also, there is the fact that the child that I was carrying belonged to Billy. Yet, Steve wanted to care for it like it was his very own child. How could I possibly say no to such an unselfish, compassionate proposal? On the other side of the coin, I too, had fallen in love…. In love with Steve and had not even been looking for love. Now, standing here before me stood the most handsome, captivating man, who was financially secure, in love with me, who wants to raise my child with me, and who wants to place the world at my feet.

"Steve…. I'm in love with you, too. And yes…. I will marry you if you want me," I uttered softly.

Steve's eyes showed pure joy. Slowly, he brought his full, moist lips down on mine. His kisses were feathery light and sent spine-tingling chills through my body. One after another, his kisses began stirring up emotions and feelings in me that had been dormant for quite some time. Some of these feelings were familiar and I succumbed to their overpowering sensations.

Steve's kiss started to become more urgent, as he explored the innermost recesses of my mouth. The waves of passion he ignited in me were thrashing and rampaging almost out of control. Just in the nick of time Steve abruptly stopped and pulled away.

"I must go Lynnie…. Right now. I'm sorry…. But if I don't leave now, I won't be able to…. Please…. Forgive me," he said in a husky tone and looking frantically into my eyes.

"I'll see you tomorrow…. I love you."

Steve kissed me quickly and hurried out the door.

Smiling contently to myself, I closed and locked the door behind Steve and leaned up against it. My mind drifted back to the terrific evening I had just had with him. I really had enjoyed myself and I was…. in love. Thinking of how flustered Steve had just gotten caused me to smile again…. especially him leaving in such a rush. It was a mischievous thought, but I just couldn't resist. Another smile adorned my face as I remembered just how close I had come to losing control. I did want Steve and the thought of being really close to him gave me goose bumps.

I knew that Steve would be patient with me under my present circumstances because he had done so countless times before about other things. I've seen that longing in his eyes many times before, but he would always manage to get it under control. Some of those times back then I wanted him to kiss me. Steve was unselfish to a fault…. He was just that kind of man. His warm, compassionate nature was a virtue in him that growing up and time did not change.

Chapter

EIGHTEEN

It was January 26th, and the cold, brisk winds howled outside. I had practically reached my ninth month and was expecting to have to go to the hospital at any time now. When I awakened this morning, I got out of bed and staggered groggily to the bathroom to wash my face. My baby had been very active much of last night and had awakened me this morning. I put on a pot of coffee and I walked to the patio to open the venetian blinds so that I could see outside and allow some light to filter in. I slid the patio door open to see how it felt outside. The brisk January air was cold and had chilled me in no time. I quickly closed the door and pulled my snuggly robe tightly around me. I grabbed a cup of coffee and sit down to enjoy it. It was just what I needed to warm me back up.

As I sat and slowly sipped my coffee, thoughts of Steve flirted with my mind. I was so glad to have his friendship. But I also knew that what Steve and I had was developing into more than friendship and that we were growing closer with each day.

As I stood up to take my mug to the sink, a terrible pain seared through my abdomen that was so intense that it caused me to sit back down. I knew instinctively that it was time…. time for my little bundle of joy to make his or her entrance into the world. I did have some concerns because my baby wasn't due for another two weeks.

I managed to keep my mind occupied by doing small chores. I was trying to wait until the contractions were closer before I bothered Steve. As the afternoon and early evening progressed, the pains became stronger with the passing time; I had to acknowledge that my child wasn't about to wait any longer to make its debut.

I concentrated on my breathing to help ease the pain. After a few hours, I called Steve and asked if he would come and take me to the hospital.

Steve got me to the hospital in record time and they wheeled me off to the delivery room, where I was prepped for birth. The labor pains were incredible, unlike anything I had ever imagined and I needed Steve. I wanted him to be there with me, holding my hand. The doctor did allow

Steve to come in the delivery room. When I saw Steve burst through the doorway of the labor-room a few minutes later, his eyes dark with worry, I knew a sudden calm, instantly knowing that everything was going to be all right now. Steve was here. That was all that mattered to me.

Steve sat down next to me, taking one of my hands in his, smoothing back the dampness of my hair with his other hand. I was sure that I must have done irreparable damage to Steve's hand as I squeezed hard on his fingers every time a contraction hit me.

And, with that one final all-consuming pain, I pushed with all the power I had within me. I laughed and cried at the same time as I heard the wail of my baby as it entered the world.

"You have a beautiful son," the doctor informed seconds later, lying the squirming bundle on my breast.

He was so beautiful…. soft and silky, with skin like caramel, wavy black hair, and his eyes dark brown as he opened them for the first time. I named my beautiful son Jarmarr because I wanted him to have Steve's middle name…. because of my love for him. Steve was thrilled at the idea.

* * * * * * *

At home, Jarmarr kept me pretty busy, from the diaper changes, his feedings, and his odd hours for sleeping. But

I soon adjusted to this regimen by sleeping whenever he slept and being awake when he was awake.

Now, I wondered if Billy would just show up and try to cause trouble for me. But he's been gone for a long time and not once had he tried to contact me. Steve reassured me that everything would be fine. He was handling the legalities of my divorce…. after all, he was an extremely good attorney.

Steve had started the divorce proceedings for me soon after I'd had the baby. I originally thought that Billy had to be here to sign the papers. Steve informed me that would not be necessary because I could get a divorce on grounds of desertion and mental and physical abuse. Since Billy wasn't here to contest it, the divorce would go along very smoothly. I was happy now and I just didn't want anything to ruin my newfound happiness.

* * * * * * * *

Within a month, my divorce from Billy became final and Steve and I began making preparations for our wedding. Actually, Steve handled most of the arrangements because he wouldn't allow me to help. He also assured me that since little Jarmarr was only six weeks old, he needed his mom more. It took very little persuasion to convince me of my priorities, because I loved Jarmarr dearly and wanted to spend as much time with him as possible. So I agreed to let Steve handle the wedding plans, except the ordering of my wedding dress, and I would stay home and care for Jarmarr.

Each passing day was wonderful and Jarmarr had doubled in weight over the past month. It was June 8th and Jarmarr just turned three months old. This was also my wedding day. Steve and I will be married at three o'clock this evening. He had asked his minister to marry us and he agreed whole-heartedly.

Jarmarr had just awakened from his afternoon nap so I bathed and dressed him. I still needed to go and pick up my wedding gown from the dress shop because it needed a few alterations. Just as I was ready to leave, the phone rang. Steve's voice echoed softly through the phone line. He said that he just wanted to hear my voice since it's considered bad luck to see the bride the day of the ceremony and tell me that my gown had already been picked up. He told me that my gown was at the church and for me to arrive there just early enough to get gorgeous. I was told that I had a surprise there waiting for me. Steve assured me that he didn't peek at my gown and that he had someone pick it up for him. After telling me once more how much he loved me, he hung up the phone.

Curious about the news Steve had just given me, I fetched my son and hurried out to the church.

I had always wanted a small, intimate church wedding and that was what Steve delivered. As Jarmarr and I entered the church, the view overjoyed me. The church was so beautiful. It was very quaint and at each stained glass window stood a pedestal with a two level, ten candle candelabra. The base of each candelabrum was adorned with a peach colored bow streaming from it that hung nearly to the floor. Each pedestal had a lovely, lighted wreath wrapped around it. Up front were many candelabras on stands with their flames delicately swaying, as they cast a mesmerizing, soft glow over the church.

As I made my way to the front, my two friends were seated on the front pew. Sam and Dee were wearing beautiful, peach colored gowns and smiling joyfully. I stood there briefly to try to gain control of my emotions because I so happy that my two friends were here.

"Hey there kiddo…. You know that you can't get married without your matron of honor," Sam resounded, lifting herself up from the pew.

"Lynnie…. We have really missed you," she added.

Dee, now standing and smiling profusely walked toward me.

"We love you Lynnie…. we couldn't miss this special day…. No way," she chimed.

The three of us embraced, as the tears flooded from my eyes.

"I'm so happy to have my best friends back," I sobbed.

Sam took a tissue and gently blotted away my tears.

"Now you are going to have to quit this stuff because

you will have me crying too," she said, with tears swelling in her eyes. Steve…. He…. He came to us and explained everything. We had all had a long discussion about you and him some time back. He convinced us of his deep love for you and also told us how long he has been in love with you. Steve was so sincere and open about feelings that Dee and I both believed in him whole-heartedly. This is the reason that we had not visited with you very much. We wanted to give the two of you the time to connect and grow closer. Dee and I could tell from his wonderful and gentle temperament that he would be a great man for you. He told us about how close you and he had become, how much he loved and cherished you, and that the two of you have known each other since high school. And he also told us about the birth of your baby, about how much you had missed us and he invited us to your wedding," Sam replied, still trying to choke back the tears.

"Dee and I both agreed…. That this was our chance to make things right again between us. We…. we wouldn't have wanted to miss your wedding for anything," Dee stammered, gazing over at me.

Lynnie…. I'm so happy that you have found someone who really loves you and little Jarmarr too. Now, you will have the closeness and family life that you deserve," Sam remarked, in a steadier tone.

"Steve is an exceptional man and he would be worth his weight in gold because of his unconditional love and compassion," Dee added.

"Thank you…... Thank you both for being my friends," I said, as my eyes began to get misty again.

I was thrilled at the fact that my friends were here to share my special day with me. I thought that I had lost their friendship forever because of Billy, but they didn't hold anything against me. They told me that after talking to Steve, they realized that my actions and attitude had come from the strong influence that Billy had over me.

"Say…... Let's get you in the back and get you beautiful for your wedding and for Steve," Sam said, grabbing me by the hand.

"We only have about an hour to get you ready."

"Yeah Lynnie…... We both are going to help you," Dee added with a brilliant smile. "Steve and Rev. Carson will be walking in here any minute…... And Steve can't see you yet."

Sam and Dee whisked me off to a room in the front of the church to get ready for my walk down the aisle with Steve.

Not very long after the reunion with my two friends, Steve and I were standing before Rev. Carson saying our wedding vows and promising to love, honor and cherish each other until death do us part. I was so elated that stray tears coursed down my face. I never would have believed that I would ever experience such love for another man. Rev. Carson had gotten to the part where we were to recite our vows to each other. Steve looked at me very lovingly as he gently placed his hand on my cheek. Tears now teased the corners of my eyes again as he began to say his vows to me.

"I, Steven Jamarr Montgomery, take Lynette Brianne Matthews, to be my wedded wife. With deepest joy I receive you into my life that together we may be one. As is Christ to His body, the church, so I will be to you a loving and faithful husband. Always will I perform my headship over you even as Christ does over me, knowing that His Lordship is one of the holiest desires for my life. I promise you my deepest love, my fullest devotion, my tenderest care. I promise I will live first unto God rather than others or even you. I promise that I will lead our lives into a life of faith and hope in Christ Jesus. Ever honoring God's guidance by His spirit through the Word, And so throughout life, no matter what may lie ahead of us, I pledge to you my life as a loving and faithful husband." As I looked into Steve's eyes, I felt overwhelming joy and love. I felt that deep within my heart, Steve would always be there and would love me unconditionally. I knew that I wanted to give him all that was within me to give because I loved him just that much.

Rev. Carson looked over to me and smiled warmly. It was my turn to say my vows to Steve and I were more than ready to begin our new life together. So I began my vow:

"I, Lynette Brianne Matthews, take you, Steven Jamarr Montgomery, to be my wedded husband. With deepest joy I come into my new life with you. As you have pledged to me your life and love, so I too happily give you my life, and in confidence submit myself to your headship as to the Lord. As is the church in her relationship to Christ, so I will be to you. I will live first unto our God and then unto you, loving you, obeying you, caring for you and ever seeking to please you. God has prepared me for you and so I will ever strengthen, help, comfort, and encourage you. Therefore, throughout life, no matter what may be ahead of us, I pledge to you my life as an obedient and faithful wife."

A stray tear creased down my face as Steve reached out and took my hands. Rev. Carson asked if anyone had just cause as to why we should not be joined, that they should speak now, or forever hold their peace. Then the pastor pronounced us man and wife and told Steve that he could kiss his new bride.

Steve and I were now husband and wife. As we turned toward Sam and Dee, we were met with very enthusiastic hugs and kisses. I could tell that they were happy for us and I know that I was thrilled beyond words. Steve and I could now begin our new life together.

Chapter

NINETEEN

After the wedding ceremony, Sam, Dee, and I chatted for a while. Most of our conversation was on things in general, but we also caught each other up on other events in our lives.

Sam and Dee began talking about Steve. They were happy for me because they felt that Steve was really good for me. Unlike Billy, they felt that Steve was a compassionate, sensitive man, he wasn't controlling, and he didn't only think of himself.

Sam and Dee each hugged me and gave me their blessings. I was so glad to have my friends back into my life because I had missed them terribly during the times that

I was with Billy. We all cried joyful tears of contentment for my marriage to Steve.

"Enough of the waterworks," Sam spoke, blotting a stray tear from her face. "Well Lynnie…. It's time for that honeymoon wouldn't you say?"

"Where are you two lovebirds going for your honeymoon?" Dee asks enthusiastically.

"Well-l-l-l-l-l…. uh-h-h…. I….

"Jamaica," Steve interrupted, his arms encircling my waist.

"We're spending 5 days and five nights there."

"Wow!" Sam exclaimed. "Jamaica! I've always wanted to go to Jamaica!"

"That's really exciting," Dee added. "Don't do anything I wouldn't do you guys," she remarked, with a mischievous glint in her eyes.

"Dee and I will keep Jarmarr for you while you are away on your honeymoon," Sam offered intently.

'We sure will." Dee chimed in. "We just want the both of you to enjoy each other and not worry about anything."

"Are you two sure about this," I asked, showing a little hesitation.

"Why of course…. Don't be ridiculous Lynnie," Sam reassured.

"Really…. It's no problem. We have your number where you will be staying so that we can call if needed. We'll see you one week from today, okay?" Dee remarked.

Steve and I took a commercial flight out that evening. We arrived at the Santo Domingo airport in almost three hours, and we took a smaller plane out to the Jamaican Isles. We arrived at our destination, the *Breezes Montego Bay Resort,* in less than an hour and were greeted by the natives with flower wreaths, hugs and kisses. Two native bellboys lead us to our cabin and stayed just long enough help us get settled.

"Hope that you enjoy your stay with us," said one of the young men. "I am Milak and this is Marques," he said in a very courteous accent. "If we can be of any assistance, please let us know."

"Thank you very much Milak," Steve said, as he tipped each one and shook their hands.

Steve stopped just outside the cabin door and told one of the guys something in a hushed tone. An enormous smile graced his youthful face. Steve slipped him another bill and patted him lightly on the shoulder. The young man rushed off and Steve closed the door and turned to face me, sporting a crooked grin.

"Well-l-l-l, Mrs. Steven Jarmarr Montgomery…. My beautiful, loving wife," Steve recited. "We are finally alone at last."

I stood there momentarily, as my eyes took in the marvelously built physique of my handsome husband. His dark eyes seemed to draw me deep within them. Our long awaited time has finally arrived. A warm feeling rushed over my body, as Steve pulled me closely to him. My arms encircled his neck, as he gently planted soft, moist kisses on my awaiting, eager lips. His kisses radiated waves of erotic passion that had every nerve in my body lit up. My body seemed to just melt into Steve, as he awakened all of my dormant desires that had long been in a state of suspension. My heart had started racing, as I succumbed to Steve's touch. As my dress slipped down my feverishly, anticipating body, Steve swept me off my feet and placed me gently on the bed. As our bodies fused together, Steve's urgency was rapidly rising, as my body was almost to explode in need of fulfillment. The uncontrollable fires of passion were coursing through my body. Just when I felt that I could no longer bear the anticipation, Steve entered me. As we rode the waves of sheer ecstasy, our bodies would rise and fall with each rhythmic thrust. As our rhythm quickened and our breathing became labored, we brought each other over the brink of heightened marital bliss. Steve held me so close and so tightly, as we lay interlaced in each other's arms; our bodies still moist from our consummated union. He kissed me ever so gently on the forehead.

"Lynnie…. Sweetheart…. I love you. You have made me the happiest man in the world today. I promise to always be a loving husband and give Jarmarr and you the very best that I can give. This is forever baby," Steve spoke softly.

Lying there wrapped in my gentle husband's arms I felt love and security that I had not experienced in what seemed like ages ago. I know now that I had a man who would be there for my son and me and would always love us.

* * * * * * *

After a wonderful night of wedded bliss, I awakened to Steve leaning over me and gently brushing his hands across my cheeks.

"Good morning Mrs. Montgomery.... You are breathtakingly beautiful.... I love you very much."

"I love you too, Mr. Montgomery," I uttered softly lacing my fingers behind his neck.

We shared a tender, loving kiss that sent a warm, tingly sensation over my entire body.

"I brought you breakfast, honey," Steve said, getting up off the bed.

When I sat up in bed, there was a cart standing there that had everything on it for breakfast.... Juice, toast, milk, scrambled eggs, coffee, bacon, ham, biscuits, pancakes, and hash browns. In the middle of all this food stood a long, slender vase and within it was a single red rose. Steve placed a tray over my lap and bent down and gave me a quick kiss.

"Eat up sweetheart, while I shower and change," he spoke, grinning happily. I'll be right out.... So save some for me, okay," he teased.

I ate while listening to Steve humming merrily in the shower. He was ecstatic over our marriage and I was too. We were both in love and I felt that we stood a magnificent chance at happiness.

* * * * * * *

Steve and I had the most wonderful time in Jamaica. There were just so many fun things to do here. We decided to get a villa and experience the many pleasures that it offered. One of the best pleasures of staying in a villa is the food. We learned that it is an excepted fact in Jamaica that the best food in the island is prepared by the villa cooks. When you first arrive at your villa, you let your cook know your culinary preferences. This will help her in planning your menus and selecting cooking methods and seasonings.

First on our agenda of recommended attractions was to visit Ocho Rios and go to the *Dunn's River Falls*. Steve and I relaxed on the beach, splashed in the waters at the bottom of the falls, and dropped into the cool pools higher up between the cascades of water.

Next on our list was the *Rockland's Bird Sanctuary* in Montego Bay. It was a wonderful experience to have these rare hummingbirds with their long tails land on your hands. The drive itself was a fun adventure. Once we got there, it really was like a little *Eden*. If you call ahead, they will set up the feeding area for you. It was amazing to see the hummingbirds come flying to you and perch on your finger for a drink. Having a hummingbird sit on my finger was heart stopping…. Just to have such a living jewel get so up close and personal with you with their bright green breast, flowing streamer tails and vivid red beak.

The next stop for Steve and I was *Alfred's Ocean Palace* in Negril. We wanted to experience the nightlife here and enjoy a night out on the town. This restaurant/bar offered a genuine cultural experience, featuring the freshest seafood the Caribbean had to offer and nightly shows. It was "OFF THE HOOK!" The crowd was lively and the performers were fantastic. I wish that Sam could have been here because there were really fine men everywhere, and there was lots of partying. The bartenders were friendly, and they made nice refreshing drinks with that island bang! Alfred's is the place to party.

Our five-day honeymoon went by much to quickly, but we did get an opportunity to visit other attractions before we left such as *Doctor's Cave Beach, the Dolphin Cove, Y. S. Falls, Rose Hall Great House, the Blue Lagoon,* and the *Milk River Mineral Baths* where we got to sit in the thermal bath. We also visited many Landmarks and Historic sites such as *St Ann's Bay Fort, Fort Lindsay, Fort Charlotte, Savanna-la-mar Fort* and several others.

Steve and I had one more night to enjoy our exotic paradise. We dressed that evening in semi-formal wear for an outdoor concert that was given each Saturday night. We dressed and went to concert. There was a great Reggae band playing and Steve and I danced under the stars until it was very late. The two of us were already in love, but here you could very easily be manipulated into a romantic mood. Looking into Steve's eyes as we danced made a warm rush sweep over me. He kissed me lightly on my lips and then along my neck, as he whispered softly.

"Let's go to our villa Mrs. Montgomery."

The night atmosphere was slightly breezy and warm and smelled of fruit and flowers. The walk back to our villa was very enjoyable as we strolled leisurely hand in hand.

Once we were at our villa, and upon stepping inside, I was totally mystified by the many candles that were placed selectively in different areas of the room. It gave the room a mesmerizing, hypnotic effect. Steve urged me toward our bedroom. Upon entering the room, our bed was covered in rose petals and there were flowers all about the room. Two bottles of champagne on ice sat in a bucket on one side of the bed accompanied by two long stemmed glasses. There was a beautiful bowl with all types of fruit sitting on a table on the other side of the bed. Finally, there was wonderful, romantic music playing that echoed softly about the room.

Everything is so beautiful Steve," I said enthusiastically.

Steve pulled me near and placed a gentle kiss on my lips. Steve cupped my face in his large, but gentle hands.

"You're so beautiful Lynnie. None of the things

in this room could come close to your natural beauty Mrs. Montgomery," he murmured, his eyes caressing my features.

Steve touched my lips to my forehead, ruffling the dark curls there with his warm breath. I closed my eyes, curling my fingers into his soft shirt.

His lips touched my eyelids and I could feel his smile. The faintest kisses on the tip of my nose made me smile in return, though I didn't open my eyes.

As he brushed his lips against my cheek, I arched into him like a cat, hungry for more of his touch.

He slid his open palms slowly down my back, his skin warm through my thin slip dress. "Tell me you want me."

"Yes." The word was little more than a sigh.

"Tell me."

"I want you."

"Lynnie." He crushed my mouth beneath his, no longer gentle or teasing. I wouldn't have complained had he given me the chance.

He slid the tiny spaghetti straps of my dress off my shoulders and down my body letting it drift to the floor.

My cheeks warmed, as I stood there clad before him. Murmuring his pleasure, Steve stroked his hands from my throat to my hips, pausing to cup my breast in his palms, to span my waist with his fingers. I stood still, my hands clenched at my sides, basking in his sensual admiration, burning wherever he touched me.

"Lynnie." Steve's voice was thick, disturbed, his gaze hot on my sensitive, hard-tipped nipples. "My God, Lynnie, you're perfect."

Steve's mouth was seeking mine again, as he pulled me in closer to him. I tipped my head back and gave myself wholly to his kiss, trembling at the sensation of being nude in arms, his clothing brushing my sensitized skin. The room was cool, and a breeze from somewhere in the room skimmed over my back. I shivered in aroused response. I had never seemed more deeply aware of my sexuality as I have been with Steve.

Suddenly impatient with the fabric between us now, I reached for the hem of his shirt, and Steve helped me to remove it. The differences in our height put his nipples within easy reach of my mouth. I touched the tip of my tongue to one tiny point and was rewarded by his sharp inhale.

"You are the perfect one, Steve," I said artlessly, smiling up at him.

He groaned and pressed me into the bed beside us, reaching for the snap of his jeans even as he followed me down. "Lynnie…. I want you so badly," he muttered, his mouth at my breast. "I've never needed anyone this badly. God, Lynnie, what are you doing to me?"

I couldn't answer. I could only arch helplessly upward when he tugged me deeply, firmly into his mouth, the movements of his lips and tongue drawing a faint cry from my throat. I was aching, swollen, hot, and the hand he slid between my legs offered only partial satisfaction. I wanted more, needed more, longed to feel him so deep inside that he'd never want to leave me, could never be taken away from me.

With a desperation that had been in solitary for so long, I rolled with him across the bed, my hands as wild, as greedy as his, my mouth as hungry, as avid. Neither of us could say a coherent word, so we spoke through skillful touches and deep, wet kisses, through broken murmurs and ragged sighs.

My heart pounded frantically in my chest, as Steve settled between my legs and as I shifted to accommodate him. Steve's eyelids closed just for a moment, his face exhibiting sheer pleasure and delight. He opened his eyes again so that he could watch me as he entered me slowly, with so much passion I felt as if I were on the verge of tears. He took his time filling me with long, slow strokes. His slow movements caused him to hit my sensitive spot continuously. He gave me orgasm after orgasm until I just couldn't stand it anymore, but he was still hard. In pushed him unto his back and stroked his pulsating member with my hands.

Throwing my leg across his hips, I straddled him and guided him back inside me. I rode Steve slowly, letting every inch of him enter me before moving back up. I took my time and enjoyed giving him the slow love that he had given me. I had gotten so used to the fast and rough loving that Billy near the end had given me, which was just a few of the times that we did have sex. Steve showed me that slow loving was just as good. Once again, my body was brought to orgasm, but this time, Steve exploded with me.

I lay in Steve's arms for a long time afterward, my cheek cradled in the hollow of his shoulder. I rested a hand on his muscular chest and concentrated on counting the heartbeats beneath my palm, pleased that it took a while for his rapid pulse to slow. I wasn't the only one overwhelmed by the powerful intensity of our lovemaking.

Steve pulled me more firmly into his arms.

"I love you Lynnie."

"Lifting my head to so that I could gaze into his dark, sensuous eyes, I replied, "I love you too Steve."

In Steve's arms, I felt secure in all that he said. I believe that we will be happy for a long time to come.

Snuggling my cheek back into his shoulder, we both drifted off to a blissful sleep.

* * * * * * *

The next morning Steve and I still had some time before we were scheduled to leave our paradise. We decided to share a shower and put on something cool and breezy and hit a few more sights before we left. Over breakfast we discussed the places that we wanted to visit. We chose to visit the *Firefly* and to take a ferry across to the beach on Sandals Cay, a private island just off the Sandals Royal

Caribbean Resort.

Our visit at the Firefly was wonderful. It was the home of playwright Noel Coward, but now is a museum offering spectacular views of the coast. Steve and I marveled the wondrous views of the coast and took many pictures before leaving this historic home and Specialty museum.

Our final destination was to visit the beach on Sandals Cove. The Sandals Royal Caribbean divided their beach into several smaller beaches through the placement of rocks, which gave us the feeling of privacy as we listened to the waves gently crashing to the shore. The resorts' gardens had well manicured lawns. As Steve and I strolled through the garden, we saw a peacock and a peahen…. They were truly a delightful sight.

At Sandals Cove, we enjoyed the exotic, private, secluded beach features of a pool with a swim-up bar and an authentic Thai restaurant where some of the dishes are rumored to be aphrodisiacs, and we enjoyed sunbathing *au naturel*! The sweet scent of tropical flowers wafted in the breeze and the water was so clear and blue that we were tempted to take a plunge.

Steve and I dined at the Thai restaurant and were treated to the legendary "Royal Touch Service."

After dining, we took a stroll in the garden. The elegant arches, dramatic porticos and picturesque promenades set the stage for a gracious escape to a more charming era. Time seemed to move at a leisurely pace, as we strolled the grounds of this stately English manor romantically set amid the lush natural beauty of Jamaica.

Steve and I made two final, unscheduled stops some stores at the Kingston Hotel…. one that sold resort wear, woodcarvings, and souvenirs. The other store was *Things Jamaican* that was a workshop and store that carried woven straw items like sandals and custom-made rugs. We picked out some gifts items for Sam and Dee.

Our week of heavenly paradise had come to and end much too quickly, but Steve and I had to return home. I had also really missed Jamarr and was anxious to see him again. After we packed our belongings, it was time to go.

As we were leaving, I paused momentarily and gave the room a once over glance.

"Don't look so sad sweetie…. We'll come back again," Steve said, reaching for my hand.

Looking into Steve's loving eyes and grabbing hold of his hand, I replied, "Okay…. Let's go."

I knew at that very moment that my experience here would be one that I would cherish always.

Steve and I boarded our plane and were headed back to the states. From above, I took one last look over our island paradise and admired all of its natural beauty…. The beautiful, blue waters, the lush foliage, and the white sand beaches. It definitely was a place that I'd love to come back to again. To be in love and spend time in such a place was a mesmerizing and magical experience.

Observing me closely and seeing the sadness come over me; Steve leaned over and pulled me into his arms.

"Sweetheart, we can come back each year to celebrate our anniversary. Don't look so sad. I don't ever want to see sadness adorn this lovely face. There is nothing that I wouldn't do for you Lynnie and I will spend the rest of my life showing you just how much you mean to me."

Steve gently kissed me and I felt as though I had the all of the security and love that I had always wanted. Finally, after so many years of being taken for granted and abused, I have a man now who really loves me…. unconditionally.

Chapter

TWENTY

Seventeen Months Later

Steve and I were happy and life was good. Though Charleston lacked the tropical appeal of Jamaica, it still more abundantly maintained and boasted its southern charm.

Steve's law practice was thriving. He was an excellent attorney and was sought after for his expertise on a continual basis. Jamarr had kept me busy over the past eleven months because he was walking now and was getting into everything. Right now he was napping and it gave me some free time to do a little housework.

It was a quarter past one in the afternoon and I

was going about my usual routine of housework. An overwhelming thought coursed through my mind. I felt as though there was still something that my life lacked. Yes, my life had been wonderful since Steve entered into it I told myself, but my life still seemed to have something missing from it. Thoughts of my career were resurfacing and I had not had these thoughts in quite some time. These memories of continuing my education had lain dormant in my mind for such a long time since Billy had mentally forced me to put them there and abandon them. I had not had the opportunity to try to attain my bachelors' degree in Business Administration. Getting my degree had been a long time goal of mine for a long time. I had placed my career on hold when Billy and I had first gotten married. The two of us had agreed that it would be best if I waited to continue my education until he had gotten better rooted in his position in the company. For one reason or another something always came up to prevent me from going back to school.

Momentarily, my conscious trailed back to how Billy had treated me --- all of his lies, manipulation, and both emotional and physical abuse. Billy had grown to be such a self-indulged, selfish person that he would not even consider the feelings of others or mine. He would just bulldoze right over you if you got in his way.

The ringing phone intruded on my thoughts and

snapped me back into reality.

"Well hello sweetheart," a soft-spoken voice echoed through the line. "How about a late lunch?"

Hi honey," I said, breaking into a huge smile. "I'd love to do lunch, but could you give me about fifteen minutes to freshen up?"

"Of course baby, but you always look beautiful to me…. even when you are doing housework. I just love you the way you are."

"Have Jamarr ready too and we can have a little picnic in the park. I'll take care of the food. The two of you just be ready to go when I arrive, okay? Love you honey!"

Steve hung up and I my face adorned an enormously happy smile, as I thought of how lucky I was to have him. No woman could ask for a more thoughtful, loving husband. The fact that he's all mine still sometimes seem unreal.

Eagerly, I hurried to the bedroom to change into something more appropriate for our outing. As soon as I had finished dressing Jamarr awakened, so I put him on a more comfortable outfit.

In a few moments, Steve breezed in. "Is everyone ready for a picnic at the park?"

Jamarr toddled over to Steve and he scooped him up into his arms. "I have everything in the car, so are we all ready to go?"

Jamarr clapped his hands together and smiled a real big smile.

"We're ready Mr. Montgomery," I said playfully. "Let's go."

Our time at the park was so enjoyable. We found a nice spot under a big elm and spread out a blanket. Jamarr was enjoying romping all around. The park was filled with birds, squirrels, ducks, and swans. There was a cool moderate, post-summer breeze blowing and the air was fragrant with smells of lilacs. Steve and I chatted as we enjoyed our fried chicken with all the fixings.

Steve's soft, brown eyes showed a little anxiety and concern, as he looked at me. I wondered if anything was troubling him at him…. maybe a difficult client or an awkward case.

"What's wrong Steve," I asked uneasily, resting my hand on top of his.

I had not ever seen Steve appear so apprehensive and uncertain. He was always so sure of himself because he radiated confidence and assurance. It was this confidence and assurance that had sustained me through my ordeal with Billy when he deserted me. I don't believe I would have survived it if it had not been for my darling Steve. I had not seen this worried look on his face since back then.

"Honey…. come on…. tell me what's worrying you."

"Lynnie…. I will never want anything more than for you to be happy. You know this already; at least I hope that you do."

"Of course Steve," I replied, even more concerned now.

"Didn't you tell me once that you had intentions of going back and finishing school?" He asked steadily.

"Why yes…. I did…. I mean…. I would like a chance to go back to school. The times that I had asked Billy about going back to school, he always had some rational justification why I couldn't at that time. Over time, I just dismissed the idea all together.

Steve studied my face very tenderly, then took my hand and gazed at me ever so lovingly.

"Baby, you are a very beautiful and intelligent woman. You are totally wasting your talent and potential. I love the fact that you take excellent care of the house, your son and me. But I want you to consider going back to school and get your degree. This is a dream of yours and I know that I will be extremely proud of you because I know that you can do it. Mrs. Montgomery can do anything that she puts her mind to," Steve boasted.

"Do you really believe that I could --- I mean with Jamarr --- Who would care for my ---

Steve silenced my appeals with a shower of tender kisses.

"I'm not taking no or maybe for an answer either," he insisted.

Jamarr and I will be just fine. He's a year and a half and I'm absolutely crazy about him. The two of us get along great. Now…. Fall classes will be starting soon and I would like to see you there, okay? Come Monday morning,

I would like for you to march your pretty little self right down to the registration office and get signed up."

Steve smiled the most wonderful smile. I fell into his arms with tear-filled eyes because I knew I had a man with a heart of gold and who loves *me*. What more could I possibly need or want.

At that moment, I knew beyond any doubt, that Steve would always stand by me. In Steve's arms I felt secure in all that he said. I believe that we will be happy forever. I know that my son could not have a better father figure than Steve.

A comforting thought eased through me as I remembered how good Steve had been with my young son. O could both sense and see that the love and patience he has with Jamarr whenever the two of them are together. He has been the only father my son had known since Billy abandoned us since before our son's birth. There were times when Steve didn't realize I was there, and I watched with admiration, as he attended to Jamarr. I could see the love in his eyes when he held him in his arms. He would tell him how he will always be there to care for him and watch him grow up.… How he will teach him to play football, baseball, and basketball.… And how he will teach him to fish and all of the things that fathers did with their sons.

At that moment I realized how great of a father Steve would be and that it would be an honor to have a child with him. It would be great if Jamarr had a younger sibling, a little brother or sister, to have under foot and to occasionally get into mischief. A baby with Steve would be a blessing of the love we have for each other. I was simply ecstatic that God had finally blessed me with the love of such a good man. Also Jamarr now had the father he so rightly deserved.

Registration for fall classes was scheduled to begin at the beginning of next week. Now that my dream of going back to school was about to become reality, I was beginning to become anxious. Though, as excited as I was about returning to school, I was a little apprehensive about whole thing. I had been out of my classes for so long and I had to find a way to settle my nerves and build up my courage to tackle the hard work that I was about to begin.

Of course Steve wasn't going to stand for me to be doubtful of my abilities and he gave me all the moral love and support that I needed. He was my anchor and had been for a long time. I knew deep down that with the love of my family, I would be capable to achieving anything.

The next week, I did register for my classes at Charleston Southern University. After speaking with my advisor, I knew what classes I needed to pursue in order to achieve my goals.

Chapter

TWENTY ONE

September finally arrived and I had begun my classes. The season was climatic for the fall of the year because of the lower humidity and temperature. Since this was my first day of classes, I was just a little nervous. I had been out of the school environment for a long time and had to make the adjustment to this life and atmosphere again. I also worried about being an older student than many of my classmates. After attending a few classes, my nerves were put at ease because there were many older students there. I became fast friends with many of my classmates and as time progressed, we formed study groups and met at each other's houses. But I also got a lot of assistance from Steve.

Steve was wonderful with my son Jamarr during the times I needed to hit the books. He'd take Jamarr on exciting outings somewhere. My son would be so high-strung when they returned that he could barely tell me about it.

Steve also took me out to dinner at a nice restaurant to celebrate when I passed my exams. Later at home I would be treated to an erotic massage that always seemed to end up taking on a life of its own.

The last semester of classes was nearing a close and I was studying extra hard to prep for my finals. I had actually done well throughout both semesters and was confident that I would past all of my exams and graduate with honors. I studied very hard because I wanted to do my best. Steve made sure that I knew all of my study questions because he would test me after I had studied. I surprised myself at the ease in which I had progressed in my studies. Though it had been such a long time since I'd been in class, I excelled with minimum effort. I got full support from Steve and he helped with Jamarr and the chores to allow me study time. I aced each and every one of my exams, with continued coaching from my loving husband.

Steve and I had become even closer during this time because he never let me give up on anything. There were times when I felt I would not make it, but Steve was always there with warm affection and support.

This school year had gone by so quickly. I had only

needed one year of prerequisites to get my four-year degree in Business Administration.

I was so excited about my up-coming graduation. Sam, Dee, and I went shopping at Northwood Mall. At Dillard's, we found lots of great outfits. This was my treat for doing so well in school. Sam and Dee sold me on a sexy; little red dress that they said was "*me.*" The dress was gorgeous and it accentuated all of my ample curves. My friends also picked out accessories…. a nice pair of matching pumps…. a classy purse…. and a beautiful necklace.

When my friends and I left the mall, they informed me of an appointment they had made for me at the beauty salon to have my hair and nails done.

On the way home, Sam and Dee told me that we were going dancing tonight at Club Habana and that I should be ready by 8:00 p.m. Without any suspicion on my part and without my knowledge, my two friends, along with Steve, had been planning an outing for me.

When I got home, Steve had already arrived. Sam and Dee walked in with me.

"Honey I'm home," I said, walking through the living room.

Jamarr ran into the room yelling excitedly.

"Mommy…. Mommy!" Jamarr resounded, rushing into my awaiting arms.

When he saw Sam, he started hopping up and down with excitement.

"Auntie Sam…. Auntie Sam! Are we going to do something fun?"

"Of course we are sweetie," Sam said, smiling broadly. "That's why I'm here."

I turned and looked at Sam in awe because I thought that the three of us were going dancing tonight.

"What are the kids talking about Sam?"

"Lynn…. This is a treat Dee, Steve and I helped to plan for you in celebration of your graduation. Steve asked if I could keep the kids tonight so that he could take you out. I was more than happy to oblige…. Besides, you two deserve this time together. Dee and I wanted to contribute to the cause, so we decided to spring for the beauty salon treatment."

I was so touched by my friends and Steve's gestures of appreciation that I almost cried.

"You guys are too much," I said, hugging my friends.

Suddenly Steve entered the room smiling mischievously.

"So-o-o-o…. what did I miss?"

"I'm going to Auntie Sam's house Daddy," he exclaimed, hopping up and down.

"That's right baby boy…. And you'll have lots of fun," Steve replied in a whimsical tone.

"Come on honey…. Let's get a move on. We have a lot of fun things to get started on," Sam said, taking Jamarr by the hand.

I kissed our son on his way out of the door. and closed the door behind them. I then turned to Steve, who displayed a mischievous smile and a raised brow.

"You know…. You are too much Mr. Montgomery. You were planning this all along weren't you?"

"I'm guilty as charged," Steve said, as he approached me. "And I'll do it again for my beautiful wife," he said, taking me by the hand.

Steve and I shared a passionate kiss as he embraced me tightly. Steve's kiss made my entire body tingle. He ended the kiss, loosened the embrace, and playfully slapped me on the behind.

"You go and get gorgeous…. Not that you can really top your already gorgeous self. I want to take you dancing tonight."

"Okay sweetie," I said, blowing him an imaginary kiss.

I showered and dressed in record time and was standing out on the patio when Steve came out. He abruptly stopped dead in his tracks, as he very lovingly admired me.

"My…. My…. My! You're a vision to behold Lynnie," he said softly.

Steve walked over and kissed me lightly on the cheek.

"Are you ready to go sweetie?"

"Of course," I said with a sensual smile.

Steve treated me to dinner first at Robert's. Robert's is one the most unusual restaurants in town and one of the best and most exclusive. The restaurant was definitely a winner in my book. It was just the place for intimate dinners. There was music playing from a pianist. Each dish that we've ever eaten has been delightful in flavor, ranging from sea scallops mousse in a Maine lobster sauce as an appetizer, to very tender, rosy duck breast in a yellow pepper cream sauce. Their garnishes are especially tasty, including roasted red pepper or hot fried eggplant.

Tonight, Steve and I will dine on smoked salmon in rosemary and butter sauce, tossed salads in a homemade vinaigrette, zesty mixed greens and vegetables. For dessert, Steve and I had the best and richest chocolate cake in Charleston, which is served with vanilla sauce, strawberries, and almond praline.

After dinner, Steve and I went to Henry's, a popular dance club in Charleston. A live band was playing very up-beat dance music. Steve whisked me onto the dance floor. We had so much fun that we danced the night away.

Things were tapering down at the club and the large crowd had slightly thinned out. The band that had been playing had been gone an hour or so and they had been playing taped top-40 music. Steve and I had been sitting and relaxing and just enjoying making small talk. A slow love song started to play. It was a song from a soulful 80's group called Dynasty and the song was *"I've Just Begun to Love You."*

Steve looked at me so very lovingly. He smiled that wonderful smile of his, pushed back his chair, and stood up before me.

"May I have this dance?"

I gazed into my husband's eyes and allowed him to lead me to the dance floor.

Steve placed his strong arms around my waist and held me closely, as we began to sway to the tone of the music. Steve leaned down and placed a feathery kiss on my awaiting lips. We became totally lost in each other as we slowly moved to the music… like there was no one here but the two of us.

As the music neared its end, Steve looked deeply into my eyes.

"I love you Lynnie…. very much. Let's go home."

Looking into Steve's eyes, I felt all the security and love that my heart and soul could hold. I had the love of a man who absolutely adorned me. Steve had made me see through his unwavering love, that wherever he was, I was home.

* * * * * * *

Steve also encouraged me to go for my Masters in Business Administration. I was a little reluctant at first because I felt so guilty for Steve having to keep up much of the responsibilities at home. He had been so understanding and wonderful with caring for Jamarr and giving me help and support with my studies. Steve assured me that what he had done and what he will continue to do is because he loves me. I did know that he Steve loved me because both his ways and actions exhibited his unwavering, unconditional love and affection.

After graduating with a bachelor in business administration and with a gentle, loving nudge from Steve, I went back for my masters' degree. Classes were a little more challenging than before, but with a lot of hard work, I did it.

* * * * * * *

I was now approaching graduation and all of the long, hard work was about to pay off. Jamarr was going on four years old and was growing like a weed. I had done so well in my classes that I had been exempted from taking the finals. This was a very exciting time for me because I was about to graduate with my Masters in Business Administration. I was proud of my accomplishment. The journey was long and hard on the way to this point, but somehow, I had achieved it.... With the support of my wonderful husband Steve.

I have to go to the college today to order my cap and gown. I'd prepared a big breakfast and had sent Steve merrily on his way. Jamarr and I went to the campus together. He smiled cheerfully, as he looked up at me while my head was being measured for my cap. When I was done with that task, the two of us visited the mall. Steve had told me to buy a nice outfit because he wanted to take me someplace special to celebrate my achievement.

Later that afternoon as Jamarr napped, I treated myself to a long, relaxing, fragrant bubble bath. I felt that the bath would help to relax me because I was so hyped up thinking about graduation and the speech I would have to deliver.

A proud smile adorned my face as I allowed myself to sink slowly into my hot bath. As my senses and body succumbed to the delicate fragrance of lilac and the warmth of the water, my mind journeyed to Steve.... my sweet, loving husband. I owed a great deal of my success to him. If I had not has his love and support, I don't know how I would have ever made it.

Steve took me to a very elegant restaurant where he wined and dined me with candlelights and the whole works. He told me how proud he was of me and also how happy he was to have me as his wife.

Later, when Steve and I got home, our lovemaking was so sweet and sensual. It was as though it had reached a new level of existence, as we lay embraced in each other's arms.

Graduation ceremonies went off without a hitch and my speech got a standing ovation. This was one of the happiest moments of my life. I had attained my goal of getting my degree. My classmates and I threw up our caps and yelled with great enthusiasm at our victories.

Chapter

TWENTY TWO

Steve seemed to be acutely aware of my ambitions and he wanted me to have my all of my heart's desires. He loved me and wanted me to be happy and feel secure. My love for Steve had grown just as strongly for him as his love was for me. I guess that this was why it only took a gentle, loving nudge from him to get me to go back to school and get a Master's degree in Business.

After graduation, I used the two and a half months to spend quality time with my family and friends. Enjoying my family and friends was a very nice break from my past rigorous studies.

Jamarr, Steve and I spent lots of time at the park, at

the Kids Theme Park, and plenty of time just relaxing at home together.

After Jamarr had gone to bed, Steve and I got to have our on private time. Much of the time we would just cuddle up on the sofa and watch mystery movies and Star Trek episodes.

When I wasn't spending time with my family, Steve suggested that I should spend some with Sam and Dee, my two best friends. We got a chance to go out to eat, went shopping and just hung out together without me fearing mental and physical abuse.

Today, my friends and I had decided to go to Sermet's Corner for brunch on this particularly beautiful, May summer day. I had kind of influenced them to eat at Sermet's Corner because I enjoyed the large windows overlooking the bustling intersection. The food was great here too.

The three of us seated ourselves where we would have a great window view of the intersection.

"Lynnie girl…. This is a really great view," Sam said, looking in awe out of the window.

Dee quickly grabbed a menu and began looking it over.

"This place does have great food Lynn."

Just as Dee said that, a waiter approached us with a big smile with notepad in hand.

"Hello ladies…. My name is Bryan and I will be you waiter today. Are you ladies ready to order?"

"We sure are," Dee said quickly. "I want the grilled seafood cakes with the Sambuca sauce and a coke."

"I'm ready too," I said looking up at the waiter with a friendly smile. "I will have a grilled chicken salad with garlic bread and iced tea."

After the waiter finished writing down my order, he asked Sam if she was ready to order.

"I think that I have decided on what I want. I'd like the savory shrimp and scallops with the sun-dried tomatoes and a coke."

The waiter wrote down Sam's order in record time and then looked up smiling broadly.

"Will that be all for you lovely ladies?"

"Yes…. I believe that will do it…. Thanks," I said.

"Alright then," he said cordially.

The waiter turned on quickly walked away.

"This is really a great place," Dee remarked, still checking out the food on the menu.

"I wanted to spend some time with the two of you. When I went back to school, I didn't get to hang out with you guys much," I said with sentiment in my voice. "I've really missed both of you."

"Girl we've missed you too. But we understand that you were taking care of your business. Dee and I are very proud of you Lynn."

"That's right," Dee added. We are proud of you. Anyway…. You can't get rid of Sam and me that easily.

So I guess you are stuck with us for life, girl."

Both Sam and Dee got up and threw their arms around me. I thank God for sending me such great friends.

"Okay! Okay! Enough of this before I start crying all over you guys," I said with misty eyes.

The waiter was now approaching us with our orders. He placed our orders in front of us along with our utensils and drinks.

"Now if you ladies need anything else, please call on me, okay?"

"Okay, but we are fine and the food looks great. Thanks," Sam said with a polite smile.

When the waiter walked away, Sam was checking him out and smiling contently to herself as she ate her food.

"Oh-o-o …. Now he's kinds fine," Sam remarked.

"And has a cute ass too," Dee added. "I can tell Sam that you want to sample that don't you? You are so naughty girl."

"Hey, I just might have to get me a sample of that too," Sam replied with a playful wink.

The three of us had a wonderful time as we chatted, laughed, and ate our lunch. I had missed this fun time with my friends.

Then my mind drifted off to a time back when Billy and I were together. Billy didn't like my friends and didn't want be to spend time with them either. I couldn't be with them the way I am right now. Billy had kept me isolated from my friends and I was alone quite often, especially during those times when he didn't come home.

"Earth to Lynn! Earth to Lynn! Where did you go just then girlfriend," Sam said with concern. "And why the sad face?"

"Oh I'm alright. I was just thinking of a time back when Billy didn't want me to hang out with you guys and it made me a little sad."

"Lynn…. Don't sweat that stuff girl. Billy is in your past and out of your life. You have a wonderful new life and a husband now who really and truly loves and cares for you and he cares about what makes you happy," Sam said.

"Yeah Lynn…. Sam's right you know," Dee said. "Billy was an asshole and we knew that he influenced you to stay away from us. We don't hold that against you."

Suddenly, Sam's face was displaying a kind of strange, unsettling look.

"Lynn…. Can I ask you something since we are talking about Billy? I think about this sometimes and wonder how you would deal with this if it came to pass."

"What is it Sam? Go ahead and ask," I said curiously seeking a reply.

"Well…. I really don't know how to ask this question so I'm just going to put it out there, okay? What would you do if by some crazy chance Billy showed up and wanted to be back into your life."?

That question sort of threw me for a loop. I had never really entertained the thought that Billy would return so I didn't know what to say. A small lump seemed to gather in my throat at the mere thought of Billy possibly coming back into my life. I felt my face flush with uncertainty and a little fear as I allowed some thought of the possibility of Billy's return to seep through my newfound security.

"I'm sorry Lynnie…. I didn't mean to upset you," Sam said apologetically.

"Oh no…. No Sam…. It's okay…. Really! I just had never given any thought to the possibility that Billy could come back, "I said, pondering in thought.

"I honestly don't know what I would do. I guess that I will have to cross that bridge if I come to it," I said, gaining my perspective.

"I do know one thing though…. I will not be trading in the new life and happiness I have found for him even if he did return. I love Steve and he loves me," I said with confidence.

"You go girl. I would feel the same way if I were in your shoes," Sam said.

My friends and I finished our meals, left a generous tip for our waiter, and left Sermet's Corner.

After leaving the restaurant, we stopped by the Northwood Mall. It…. was…. on…. time to shop, shop, and shop some more.

We hit Dillards', Express Men, Bath & Body Works,

Belk, Claires' Boutique, Lady Footlocker, Magic Nail Spa, and Victoria Secret.

After shopping, we all went to the nail salon and got facials, manicures and pedicures. This special treatment was great and we enjoyed each and every minute of it.

The day that I had spent with friends had been wonderful. On the way home we chatted about our purchases and about when we would do this again.

As Sam pulled into my driveway, she and Dee said that we would all have to do this again soon.

I gathered my bags and stepped out of the car.

"I'll see you tomorrow Lynn. Now you hurry on it to that sexy husband of yours," Sam said with a mischievous smile. "Behave yourself."

"Girl you are hopeless," I said waving good-bye to my friends.

When I entered the house, Steve had left one lamp on so that the house would not be completely dark and I turned it off as I went pass. As I made my way to the bedroom, I could smell the heavenly aroma of lavender scented candles, which was one of my favorites. When I entered the bedroom, it was lit up strictly by candlelight, and they were placed selectively about the room. Lying in the middle of our king-sized bed was Steve.

"Hello sweetheart! I've been waiting for you. Did you and your friends have a great time?" he asked sincerely, getting out of the bed.

"Yes…. yes we did," I said, sitting my bags on the floor.

Steve approached me and placed a delicate kiss on my lips. Then he slowly began undressing me, kissing each bare area as it was exposed. He continued to undress me until I was left with only my lacy underwear. I stood there before him totally captivated in his sultry eyes and was caught up in his sensual seduction.

Steve swept me off my feet and carried me to our bed. After placing me in bed, he quickly joined me.

Steve placed his arms around me, pulled me gently to his strong, sexy body. He looked lovingly into my eyes, as he caressed my anxiously aroused body. He kissed me deeply, the left a trail of wet kisses from my face to my neck to my chest.

We paused momentarily to remove the rest of our clothing so that there would me absolutely nothing to prevent our bare skins from touching.

Steve kissed and licked my nipple, teasing me into a frenzy. My body was writhing on the bed beneath his touch. His hand was moving up and down my thighs as he continued to tease my nipples. It felt incredible. I was so excited and wanted him inside me, but I didn't want him to stop what he was doing either. I unconsciously put my hand between my legs and began to touch myself. My passion was growing rapidly as I rubbed my little jewel, and as he continued to love my breasts with his tongue.

"Oh baby! I need you." I begged.

I was on fire. Finally, he moved his body on top of mine, and I guided his pulsing member into my wet center. I exploded in ecstasy immediately as he filled me up with his manhood. My nails raked his back as his lovemaking caused me to have continuous orgasms. Sweat was pouring from my body. I tried to muffle my screams as my orgasms became stronger and stronger. He rolled over on his back, pulling me on top of him, without pulling out. I rode him slow and easy, enjoying each and every movement as I raised and lowered my body. My eyes were closed, and all I could see was Steve making love to me. Finally, Steve and I exploded together in a mind-blowing climax.

We laid together with me on top of him for a long time in silence. The only sounds that we could hear were our steady, even breathing.

"I love you Lynnie," Steve said, breaking the silence.

"I love you Steve."

I repositioned myself so that I was lying side by side with Steve. He pulled me in snuggly to his muscular body, as I settled myself into the curve of his secure arms.

As Steve's breathing changed, I could tell that he was falling asleep. I thought to myself, this was the kind of life that I had always wanted…. To be loved and have the security that I would always be loved and cared for. I know that I had this kind of love with Steve and that he would always think of my feelings and put me first.

I could feel peaceful, content sleep on its' way to claim me now. As I allowed sleep to take me, I felt secure in the fact that I had his heart and his love.

TWENTY THREE

The warm July sun was shining through the vertical blinds of the bedroom as I slowly awakened in Steve's arms. I wanted to remain in the secure and loving peace of this morning. I turned over in bed, trying to ignore the sun's call to wake up. Not to be ignored, the sun was shining into a mirror standing on the right side of the futon, reflecting a bright glare onto my sleepy eyes.

"Okay, I'm awake," I mumbled groggily to myself, as sat up and threw my legs out of bed. Satisfied with my acknowledgement of the new day, the sun dispersed its' reflection, leaving me to rub my stunned eyes. Though I wanted to move the mirror, the glare served as a useful alarm clock. I got out of bed and went over to the vanity, sat down, and picked up my hairbrush. I began brushing my shoulder-length, black hair in the mirror, and softly talked to the reflection in the mirror as to a familiar friend.

"Girl you are so lucky to have Steve. He is the best thing that could have happened to you outside of your son."

Not waiting for a reply, I continued, *"You have the love, support, and security of a great man. He's a wonderful father figure and step-father, a wonderful provider and husband."*

A satisfied smile parted my lips, as I turned and admired my handsome husband still sleeping.

I threw on my robe and went to the bathroom to wash my face and brush my teeth. Afterward, I went to the kitchen to start coffee and make breakfast.

As I prepared breakfast, my thoughts coursed to my studies. There were only a few weeks left before fall classes were scheduled to begin. The summer weeks had flown by and I really enjoyed the quality time that I had spent with my family and friends. I must make the most of the upcoming two weeks because classes start on the 19th of this month.

I had pre-registered for classes after my graduation and after being encouraged by Steve. My business advisor had informed that I only needed 30 college credit hours to attain my Masters' degree in Business Administration. If I took five requisites each semester and pass them, I could graduate next May. I knew that my husband would be right there supporting me and encouraging me.

Putting the finishing touches on my breakfast casserole, I placed it in the oven to bake.

I walked over to the vertical blinds and pulled them open. The day was beautiful outside. I slid the patio door open and a fragrant, moderate breeze stirred outside, and swallows darted about in acrobatic flight.

Suddenly, a pair of strong arms slid around my waist and feathery kisses lavished my neck.

"Good morning beautiful," a sultry, deep voice said.

As I turned around, I was totally captivated by Steve's sensual smile.

Freshly shaven and clad in lonely his boxers, he was a titillating, sexy vision to behold. His broad, muscular chest and body excited me and my body seemed to melt into his, as I stepped into his arms.

"Hello handsome," I said softly, smiling enormously. "Did you sleep well?"

"I slept like a baby," Steve said with a playful wink, as he kissed me lightly on the lips.

"Breakfast will be ready in about fifteen minutes."

"I'll go and get Jamarr up sweetie. It'll take that long to get him up and going."

By the time Jamarr and Steve had washed up and dressed, I had set the table, made pancakes and was ready to serve breakfast.

After breakfast, Steve took all of us on an all day outing. Jamarr was very excited about the pleasure excursion.

First on Steve's schedule of *family-things-to-do*, was a Charleston Carriage Ride. The ride went through Charleston, where the first shots of the Civil War were fired and where beautiful mansions and plantation homes enhance the tradition of the true south.

Steve talked and explained any questions that Jamarr or I had about the sights as we rode past them. He was very knowledgeable about history and explained everything in terms that someone as young as Jamarr could understand.

On our carriage ride, we paid tribute to Charleston's birth at Charles Towne Landing, and visited some of the highlights of the Charleston Drayton Hall, the Magnolia Gardens, and Middleton Place.

After the carriage ride, Steve took us to the White Point Gardens. It was right on the end of the peninsula facing the Cooper River and the harbor. It had a beautifully landscaped park, with shaded palmettos and live oaks, with walkways lined with monuments and other relics. The view of the harbor went out to Fort Sumter. We all enjoyed the walk along the seawall on East Battery and Murray Boulevard and slowly absorbed the Charleston ambience.

Our next stop was the Great Hall at the Old Exchange. Steve wanted Jamarr to see the Provost Dungeons where

South Carolina patriots spent their last days, and see the last remaining structural evidence of the Charleston Seawall. Steve also took us by the Audubon Swamp Garden.

We stopped our touring of Charleston momentarily to have lunch. Magnolias' was the place of choice. It had the southern hospitality and charm that kept the place buzzing day and night. Lunch was the best time for families and children.

We ordered sandwiches and saved room for homemade warm cream cheese brownies with white-chocolate ice cream and chocolate sauce.

After eating, Steve, Jamarr and I visited the **South Carolina Aquarium**. It's located on the *Charleston Harbor* and it depicted the aquatic habitats of the state from rushing mountain streams through rivers, lakes and the salt marsh, to the depths of the Atlantic Ocean. Along the way, we encountered river otters, snakes, turtles, birds, fish and sharks. The trip to the aquarium was both fun and educational for Jamarr.

Steve had one more place that he wanted to share with Jamarr -- a stop at *Hollywild Animal Park*. It was one of the most scenic and culturally diverse areas of South Carolina's Upcountry. It's nestled on 100 acres, and is home to one of the largest collections of rare and exotic animals in the Southeast. Steve chose this zoo because many of the animals there are *"ZooperStars"* of movies and commercials. *Hollywild ZooperStars* have been featured in countless commercials and all over 60 Hollywood movie productions. Some of their credits includes *The Big Chill, Prancer, Prince of Tides, Monkey Shines, Reversal of Fortune, Days of Thunder, Betsy's Wedding, Last of the Mohicans, The New Adventures of Pippi Longstockings, and The Stand."*

All of this knowledge about the animals here at this zoo was news to me because I had no idea that the smartly trained and highly intelligent animal stars came from here. Jamarr was absolutely thrilled with all of the animals and with the Outback Safari ride that we took. As we were driven through the Outback aboard the special safari bus, we all were thrilled with the adventure and excitement of being surrounded by dozens of animals, many of which would eat right out of your hands.

Hollywild Animal Park was the last stop that Steve had planned for our daylong pleasure trip. The day had been absolutely wonderful and even I had learned new things today.

Darkness had silently claimed the excitement and activities of the day. The drive home was very enjoyable too. Jamarr was exhausted from all of the excitement of the day and had fallen sound asleep. Steve and I enjoyed the scenery and chatted all the way home. The city and the night were really pretty at night and I took in everything -- the lights, the star-filled sky, and the fragrant smell of the magnolias along the street that we traveled.

Pulling into the driveway, Steve parked and lifted a

sleeping Jamarr from the back seat of the car and carried him inside, with me trailing closely behind.

Steve and I both tucked Jamarr in bed, kissed him goodnight. Then we got ready for bed ourselves.

Steve and I hopped into bed and snuggled up together with his arms enveloped securely around me. Lying in his arms was the safest, loving and secure feeling. It was very hard for me to believe that I could be this happy. My life was wonderful and I felt that this happiness and love would last.

* * * * * * *

July 19th was a beautiful day. It was the first day of kindergarten for Jamarr and my first day back to my classes at college. The past two weeks had flown by and it was time for me to hit the books again.

Steve took Jamarr to school and then went to his office and I was on my way to the college campus. Steve suggested that since Jamarr's school is closer to where his office is, he would be the one to take him to school.

I know that these two semesters are going to be very hard, but I was determined to attain my goals. O course I did have plenty of encouragement too from Steve.

When I met with my business advisor Mrs. Killion, she mapped out aims and objectives of the Masters of Business Studies. Mrs. Killion told me that the aim of the business courses were to endow students with a well developed understanding of international business and the appropriate knowledge and skills in order to obtain entry into management positions. She advised me that the courses she had planned out for me were to give me a thorough understanding of the fundamentals of business and facilitate the development of skills for business.

In order for me to enter the MBA program, I had to have a minimum Second Class Honors in a business degree, have an Honors Graduate Diploma in Business Studies, and have a primary degree with a minimum of three years experience in a business environment.

I had gotten my three years of a business environment experience during the three years of college I had taken earlier back before Billy and I had gotten married. In addition, I have the year that I just finished this past May.

The qualification for the three years in a business environment was acquired when in my earlier years of college. For three years while I was going to college back then, I worked for the Department of Human Services as an administrative assistant. I satisfied the requisite for an Honors Graduate Diploma when I had attained my bachelors' degree with honors this past May.

Mrs. Killion said that she was very proud of me to enter into the MBA program because of my honors and my fierce determination to succeed in getting my degree. I was allowed 2 years to get an MBA degree, but I had plans of putting my nose to the grindstone and getting the degree in 1 year. I knew that it would be a very challenging program with seven subjects per year and a thesis that would count for 60 credits instead of 15 credits like the other module I had to take. With all of this work ahead of me, I am still determined to reach my goal of getting an MBA.

* * * * * * *

It was spring and I had one half of my term over. So far, I had done very well and was passing all of the required modules in the program. It had been a long, hard semester and many nights I had stayed up late trying to make the deadlines for my courses. Steve was right there helping in every way that he could, supporting and encouraging me every step of the way.

The second half of the semester would be more of the same hard work as I had just previously done. The semester would be just as hard if not harder than the first half.

During this semester, I had to place a lot of focus on my thesis. This would require much research and writing in order for me to come up with some great work.

Steve told me that he would help me with my research and preparation. Even though the two of us were hard at work on my thesis, I still enjoyed time spent with him alone immensely. Steve was great at this sort of stuff because he was great at presentations, writing, and in doing research.

Sometimes his cases called for research and he had to be capable of being prepared and in presenting his cases very well. I learned a great deal from Steve over the course of my studies because he was a very knowledgeable man and had shone me so much patience during the entire time I have been in school.

* * * * * * *

The last semester was nearing a close and I had put the final touch to my thesis. Steve had gone over both of my works with me and listened attentively as I presented it.

Steve and I had been working on my thesis presentation one night when a strange awareness and revelation swept over me. Near the end of my presentation, I suddenly burst into tears.

Steve rushed by my side with a very concerned expression on his face.

"What's wrong baby?" he asked, as he lovingly lifted my hands.

Looking into his dark, sensual eyes, tears cascaded down my face.

"There is nothing really wrong sweetheart…. That's just it," I choked out.

"You have done so much for me Steve. I have never known a man that has been as patient, loving, and compassionate with me as you have been. You take care of my son as if he were your own and have been taking care of the house and chores…. you have stayed up with me through the entire duration of my attending college and helped me when I ran into snags…. you kept my spirits up during times that I was down…. you made me see that I could do this Steve…. you believed in me and you did it even during the times that I didn't have faith in myself."

"Believing in you was easy Lynnie," Steve said, looking into my eyes, as he brushed astray tear away. "You are a very intelligent woman…. And not forget -- sexy as hell. You just had lost your confidence in yourself for a while and just quit believing in yourself. I just simply allowed you to be you."

Steve put his arms around me and held me close. I felt so loved and happy…. I didn't have to pretend or be afraid to speak…. I could just be me and be accepted with open arms.

* * * * * * * *

It was the last week in April and I had just finished the last of my final exams. The only thing that was left now was for me to do my thesis. I had rehearsed it several times with Steve and he said that it was excellent, but I was so nervous about presenting it before the faculty at college.

After I was done with my last exam, I turned it in and headed for the conference room where I was scheduled to present my thesis at 1 p.m.

Steve had promised me that he would come to the college to give me moral support. Just being able to see him before I went in would give me the encouragement that I needed to get through the oral presentation.

As I rounded the last corner of the hallway, Steve was standing near the door of the conference room.

"There's my girl," he said, extending his arms to me.

"Steve…. I am so nervous."

"You will be great honey. All you have to do is have confidence in yourself. You can do this. I have all the confidence in the world in you -- I also love you very much. So you go in there and show them your stuff."

"Thanks for being here Steve," I said with a confident smile.

My thesis went off very well and I got a standing ovation from several of the faculty members, including my advisor, Mrs. Killion. They each came up and shook my hand and commended me on my in depth research, and the ease in which I gave my presentation and my professionalism.

As the last faculty member left, Steve came in displaying the biggest smile.

"I am so proud of you Lynnie. I knew that you could do it," he said with much admiration and love.

Steve gave me biggest hug. As I stood there in his arms, an amazing peace swept over me. I felt as though I could just scream the happiness that I felt at that very moment. My final dream had just come true. I had attained my Masters' degree in Business Administration.... I had the family that I always wanted -- a wonderful son and a husband who loves me dearly. I had it all.... and I'm going to hold on to it with both hands.

Chapter

TWENTY FOUR

A year later

After attaining my Masters' Degree, acquiring a job wasn't very hard. I was the administrative director/ chief operating officer of the South Carolina Federal Credit Union. My primary duties would include positively leading the Quality Improvement Process through direct reports to ensure that all actions are driven by positive member care initiatives that included maintaining accurate and complete credit files and supervising, coaching, mentoring and support of department staff to ensure their success. I was so excited about beginning my new job and assuming the responsibilities that accompanied it. This was my dream come true…. a goal that I had almost foolishly discarded if it had not been for Steve.

The first few months on the job were really a learning experience, but I seemed to progress rather nicely through the functions and obligations that came with having this position.

Though my job was demanding, I still made time for my family. Jamarr was now a second grader, Steve's practice was flourishing, and I had settled into my job very nicely. Steve and I always planned time around our busy schedules that was specifically for family and for just the two of us. Our quality time together was so important and it kept us close and in tune with each other. Our life together was going so well. We were very happy and totally committed to each other in every way. Jamarr was notably well adapted and contented and was doing terrific in school. Every aspect and everything in our lives had fallen into place…. everything was simply wonderful.

On this particular morning, I awakened feeling sick to my stomach. I rushed to the bathroom because I had a sudden urge to throw up, but I didn't and the feeling passed. I sit down for a little while until I felt certain that my stomach settled down and the nausea passed.

On the third morning, I was still having nausea and I also had occasional dizziness. As I sat and ate my crackers, a happy thought entered my mind. I wondered if maybe I was pregnant.

I scheduled an afternoon appointment to see my doctor. I took the afternoon off work and arrived at the doctor's office around 2:00 p.m. The doctor's assistant placed me in a room and acquired a urine sample. Afterward, she escorted me to another room to wait for the results of the urine sample and for the doctor. While I waited for my doctor, I nervously flipped through the pages of a magazine.

My mind trailed off to thoughts of Steve and how he might feel and react if I am indeed pregnant. I would hope that he will be thrilled at the fact that there would be a new addition to the family. I already knew that Steve would make a great father because he has been so good with Jamarr. But having his very own biological son or daughter would really change his life.

A knock on the door invaded my thoughts, as Dr. Balthrop opened the door and entered the room.

"Hello Mrs. Montgomery…. how are you feeling today?"

"I'm feeling very well Dr. Balthrop except for the occasional dizziness and nausea," I admitted. "And please, do can call me Lynnie."

"Well…. Lynnie…. the nausea will begin to let up in few weeks and so will the dizziness. The test results say that you are going to me a mom. Congratulations!" Dr. Balthrop said smiling. "I'd like to see you back in my office in three or 4 weeks" If you happen to have any problems in the meantime, please let me know. You can get with my assistant and she will schedule your next visit, okay? I will see you then Lynnie."

"Thank you Dr. Balthrop and I will schedule that appointment."

When I left the doctor's office, my head was in the clouds because the drive home went by in a blur. My mind rebounded back and forth to joyful thoughts of the new life I now carried inside of me.... thoughts of how Steve would feel about the product of the love we share.... thoughts of how happy I hope Steve will be when I give him the news of my pregnancy. I was pretty sure that he would be very happy with the news that I was carrying his child. Steve has been so good to Jamarr and I know that my son loved him.

As I turned into the driveway, I noticed that Steve had not made it home yet. So I used this opportunity to plan my surprise for the love of my life. I called my friends, Sam and Dee the share the news and to see which one of them could keep Jamarr for a little while. Sam jumped at the opportunity to spend time with Jamarr. I explained to them that I wanted to surprise Steve and have a little time alone with him. Dee was ecstatic about having another godchild to spoil rotten.

Sam came and picked up Jamarr and took him to the arcade gallery cand I weent to prepare a special meal for Steve. By the time he arrived home, I had a nice candlelit supper and soft music playing on the stereo. I greeted him with a sensual kiss that lingered momentarily. Steve's arms encircled my waist, as he drew me close.

"I love you so very much Lynnie," Steve said in a husky tone. "You are a beautiful, sexy woman," he added, gently stroking my cheek.

"I love you too honey," I murmured, craning my neck in his strong, gentle hands.

"I've prepared a special meal for us. Let's sit down and eat. I also want to share some news with you," I said leading him to the dining room.

After finishing our meal, Steve and I retreated to the den. Steve had a concerned look on his face.

"What is this news that you share with me," he said cradling my hands in his.

My eyes began to become misty, as I looked into Steve's loving face.

"Sweetheart…. I'm pregnant," I uttered abruptly. "Dr. Balthrop said that I'm about six weeks."

Steve's face seemed to become totally consumed with excitement.

"You're pregnant! You're pregnant! That means that I'm going to be a father! I'm going to be a father!" he cried with enthusiasm, as he gathered me in his arms and held me tightly.

"Baby, I love you…. I love you!" he rambled, showering me with kisses.

I was thrilled that Steve was so happy about the baby. When Sam returned with Jamarr, I explained everything to him…. that he would have a little sister or brother soon.

* * * * * * *

Time seemed to fly, as the months passed one by one. It was nearing Christmas and I was in my eighth month of pregnancy. I had gained a lot of weight and the doctor predicted that I would give birth around January 14th. Even though I had followed doctor's orders and was careful with my diet, I still had quite a bit of swelling in my feet, legs, and hands. I believe Dr. Balthrop' medical term for this swelling was toxemia. I had to remove my wedding ring because my hands had swelling too. Dr. Balthrop decided that I needed to stay off my feet as much as possible. He said to keep my feet elevated and get lots of rest. Steve made sure I rested because he checked on me throughout the day, either by calling me or coming home. During my last month of pregnancy, Steve only worked until noon.

Early one Sunday morning, about two weeks from my due date, I began having sharp pains. These pains, in the beginning, started off being quite a ways apart. Usually, Steve is home on Saturdays, but in had to go into the office for a few hours this morning. I decided not to bother him at the office and to wait and tell him about my pains when he came home. By Saturday evening the pains were about an hour apart. Since Steve had been at the office longer than he had expected, I decided to call him and let him know that I had been having labor pains. It was hard convincing him that everything was still okay for now, and that we could leave for the hospital later. Steve finally gave in and went with my judgment.

By 3 a.m., Steve had to take me to the hospital. Our little bundle of joy was just about ready for their entry into the world. Steve stayed by my side in delivery the entire time, holding my hand and whispering words of comfort.

Just over an hour later, our beautiful baby daughter, Brianna was born. She was 21 inches long, weighed 9 lbs. 5 ½ ounces, and had a head full of long, dark, wavy hair. Steve was so proud of her. He called her his little precious angel. I glowed with admiration, as I watched Steve hold our baby because I knew that he loved her more than life itself.

The happiness that I felt right now went beyond words. I felt as though my heart was about to burst open with sheer, unadulterated joy. Thinking back to the later times when Billy and I were together, I couldn't have imagined feeling this way. It just goes to show you that life has a way of balancing things out. The bad happenings of the past can lead to good things in the present. I was overjoyed that I didn't let my life slip through my fingers by living in the past. You learn to forgive the bad times and overcome the resentments. You learn to move forward and be thankful for what you do have.

TWENTY FIVE

Four years later

Spring was dawning and buds were beginning to form on many trees and shrubs. Some of these trees and shrubs had leaves and blossoms on them. The sweet smell of magnolias and lilacs caressed me, as I stepped onto the patio. I often got up early to simply enjoy the tranquil surroundings…. the smell of the sweet fragrances and the calmness of the early morning, along with my cup of coffee; this started my busy day.

Brianna was just over four years old and Jamarr was ten. I had already gotten Steve off to work and he had taken Brianna to daycare on his way to the office. Jamarr had just boarded the bus for school and I was on my way out the door when the phone rang. I turned and hurried back to answer it because I thought that it might have been Steve.

"Hello Lynnie," the voice echoed through the phone line.

The voice sounded familiar, but I couldn't quite figure out who it could have been.

Suddenly, my knees weakened beneath me.... they felt as though they would no longer support me. Emotionally shocked, I slowly eased down in a chair near the phone.

"It's me Lynnie.... your husband Billy," the voice recited again.

"B.... B.... Billy? Is this really you?" I stammered, still trying to regain control of my emotions.

"Where have you been all this time," I spoke in a more confident voice.

"I thought you were dead or something. Now, after almost ten years, you decided that you needed to give me the courtesy of a phone call? That's a bit of a long time wouldn't you say Billy?" I remarked bitterly.

"It has been a long time Lynnie, and I'm sorry for putting you through that heartache," Billy said, trying to sound regretful.

"You're sorry! You walk out of my life without any sort of explanation, and all you have to say is that you're sorry! You damn right you sorry! How could you just desert your unborn child and me like that? You never tried to call or anything…. not one word or a thought about our welfare. You know…. you're a self-centered, manipulative, inconsiderate son of a…."

"You're right Lynnie," he interrupted. "You're right. I realize now that saying, I'm sorry doesn't even scratch the surface. I mean…. I…. I just walked out of your life without any kind of an explanation for almost ten whole years."

Billy hesitated for a moment, as I fought desperately to maintain my calmness.

"Lynnie!" He spoke, his voice piercing the silence that had claimed both of us. I…. I really need to speak with you in person if that is possible. I'd rather do it face to face."

I could feel an achy thickness building up in my throat, as I pondered on how to answer the question Billy had just asked me.

"I've got to get to work," I finally managed to say. "Where can I reach you later if I decide to see you?"

Billy gave me the number to the hotel he was staying in, as I nervously jotted it down. He told me that he'd be waiting to hear from me soon before hanging up.

I stood there briefly, still holding the phone, as it hummed steadily in my ear. I could not understand all the emotions that Billy's phone call had caused.

Somehow, I managed to drive to work. My thoughts were riddled with confusion and anger, as I tried to focus on my work, but to no avail. Steve's angelic face intruded in my thoughts. I wondered how he would react to knowing that Billy was back and I knew that I had to tell Steve.

Listening to the tone of Steve's phone ringing in my ear, I rehearsed in my mind how I would break the news about Billy's return.

"Hello…. Montgomery Law Firm," his gentle, yet strong sounding voice echoed through the line.

"Hi honey," I uttered nervously.

Steve had grown to know me so well and could sense that something was wrong and he could hear it in the tone of my voice.

"What's wrong sweetie," he spoke in a soothing manner.

I paused for a second, trying to summon strength to speak again.

"You won't believe who is here. Steve…. Billy has come back. He called me this morning as I was leaving for work. I answered the phone thinking that it was probably you," I rambled. "He said that he needs to see me…. that he has something very important to talk to me about…. and he says that he wants to see his son. Jamarr has never known Billy and you are the only father he has ever known all his life.

Steve was quiet on the phone, as he patiently listened to me talk. Feeling the hostility and resentment toward Billy burning deep within me, I continued speaking, but the anger was about to spill out.

"Who in hell does he think he is anyway? Does he think that he can just walk right back into my life without one word from him in all these years? Now, he just wants to drop back into our life unannounced. I have a life now.... a new life.... without him. My life is with you Steve.... and my children. And I'm not giving up my happiness and all my triumphs because he decided to grace me with his presence again. He can just go crawl back under whatever rock he crawled out from under. He can go straight to --

"Wait a minute sweetie. Hold up for a minute," Steve broke in abruptly. "Just calm down before you work yourself into a frenzy. We can work this out. I'll cancel the rest of my appointments for today and I will see you at home, okay baby," Steve said with reassurance. "It will all be alright.... You'll see. I love you."

After talking with Steve and knowing that I had all his love and support, I felt a little more at ease. But I still didn't look forward to seeing Billy again. All of the contempt and resentment that I had felt toward him had come flooding back and I thought that I had long since put them to rest, that is, until now.

I told Mr. Sullivan, the president of the company, that I needed the rest of the afternoon off to attend to some personal business. He agreed to my request without hesitation and bid me a good evening.

By the time I made it home, Steve was already there. He had heard me drive up so he greeted me at the door. As I stepped inside our home, he closed the door softly. I fell into his massive, muscular chest sobbing uncontrollably, as he held me close. I felt so secure in my husband's arms and was so happy that we had found each other. As I looked at Steve through tear-filled eyes, his gentle hands softly wiped away my tears.

"You know Lynnie how much I love you," he said, his dark eyes gazing at me so full of love.

"You do need to see Billy so that you can finally put your past to rest."

I slightly pushed away from Steve and looked at him in astonishment at the words he had just said. Steve cleared his throat and continued to speak.

"You are a very strong lady…. You can do this and you should. I'll be right by your side if you want. As for as him seeing Jamarr…. we can all go together sweetheart…. you, Jamarr, Brianna, and I. Now, all you have to do is call him and tell him that you will see him and what time. Everything will be just fine…. It will be okay," Steve whispered softly.

I called Billy and told him that I would see him at the Hominy Grill restaurant at 5 p.m. Billy agreed with my suggestion enthusiastically. The Hominy Grill had a bar area just off from the dining area. I chose the Hominy Grill because I knew that Steve and the kids could be near me there and also the restaurant had a very nice atmosphere.

Steve, the kids, and I had arrived at the Hominy Grill a little early because Billy had not yet arrived. Steve reassured me before seating himself with the children at a table adjacent to me. I sat nervously and impatiently at the bar, occasionally glancing at my husband Steve, who would flash an assuring smile and a quick wink. This was his way of letting me know that he was there for me with love and support.

I turned on the bar stool and asked the bartender to fix me a small drink, hoping that it would maybe help me to relax. As I sat there sipping on my drink, my mind journeyed to Billy. I wondered how he might have changed, both in appearance and attitude. He used to be such a handsome and physically fit man, and I had once loved him so much. I could not imagine why he aborted our relationship and all the love we had once shared. Billy had been my world. After he deserted me, I didn't think that I could ever go on without him, much less find happiness again. I never would have thought that my heart would have had two loves because I believed that Billy and I would have been forever. Steve had shown me so much love and happiness. He was the one who had made me whole again, filling in the emptiness that I had in my heart. I found total fulfillment beyond anything I could have imagined with Steve.

"Hello Lynnie," a soft, deep voice vibrated behind me, breaking my thoughts and startling me.

I spun around on the bar stool and saw a tall, thin, man who had salt and pepper hair and a neatly trimmed mustache, who was smiling uneasily. I looked at this man in wide-eyed amazement because he didn't really look like the Billy I last remembered.

"Is this really you? Billy chimed. "Woman.... you know you look so damn good! You seemed to have hardly changed," the man continued. "You're as beautiful as ever."

"Excuse me! How do you know my name?" I spoke sharply, not recognizing the fellow standing before me.

"I don't know you! I'm afraid you have me mistaken for someone else."

Disappointment showed on the man's face, as his eyes fell on the glass that I held in my hand. He looked at me again, but this time with a more serious look on his face.

"It's me Lynnie.... Billy," he finally managed to say.

"Don't you recognize me?"

Looking into the man's face and seeing the hurt in his eyes because I couldn't acknowledge who he was, I started to see somewhat familiar traces of someone I had once known.

"Billy.... are you Billy?" I asked with uncertainty, and still gazing into his face.

Slowly nodding his head, he responded. "Yes Lynn.... this is me."

"But Billy…. If this is you…. what happened to you? You look so frail."

"I know that I look pretty bad, but I have really been through a long, gut-wrenching, ordeal over the course of ten years," he remarked, taking a seat on the stool next to me.

Billy readjusted himself on the stool, clasping his hands together in front of him on the counter.

"Lynnie…. I wasn't really myself when I walked out on you and our baby ten years ago. I had gotten mixed up with some bad people…. drug dealers.

A solemn look came over Billy's face, as he paused momentarily before continuing to speak.

"It all started out with me just getting a little high sometimes to take the edge off the stress I had from the day so that I could unwind. Then the guys that I was buying from felt I'd be an asset to them. I, on the other hand, felt that I could make some easy money. After I spent the weekend once at their penthouse, they felt I was responsible and was someone that they could trust with their money and drugs. They even gave me my own stash to sell for myself or to use if I desired. Before I knew it, I was using more and more until I began skimming off their supply and their money. That's why I stayed so edgy with you all the time…. the mood swings…. the attitude…. staying out all night and entire weekends…. the fits of anger…. the abuse I inflicted on you…. all because I had gotten hooked on drugs. I lost control of my life and myself and I didn't care about anything anymore…. not even myself. When Romeo (Roman Pierce), the top man of these drug people got wind of me taking his drugs and money, he had them set me. One night when I was at the penthouse preparing some of the drugs for a pick-up, the cops suddenly raided the house. They arrested me and carted me off to jail. I just couldn't bring myself to call you and tell you about the huge mess I had gotten myself into because I was too ashamed and afraid for you. They convicted me and I was sentenced to 15 years in prison for the drugs that they confiscated at the penthouse. The DEA decided to cut my prison time to seven years because I gave them full cooperation. The agency managed to trace ownership of the house and drugs to Romeo and some of the others. These drug dealers had intended for me to get locked up so they set me up to take the fall. Getting me locked up was payback for my taking their drugs and money. I was really very lucky…. they could have had me killed. Look Lynnie…. what I'm trying to say is that I had no choice but to keep quiet about everything. I didn't want you linked to me in any way in case those thugs had decided to try to find someone who was connected to me and hurt them just to get back at me."

Billy hesitated briefly before continuing his story, as I listened and watched in total disbelief at this man…. a man who I had once loved so very much, had dealt drugs. "Besides Lynnie…. you were actually better off without me. I had to have nearly 2 years of drug rehabilitation for that crack cocaine addiction I had. The way I treated you Lynnie was a disgrace. I still can't believe that I actually hit you."

Billy's words caught in my throat because I really did believe his story. His eyes became misty, as he gathered my hands into his. I was moved by his motives for not letting me know what had happened to him with the drug dealers and him not maintaining any contact with me all this time. But I also realized that Billy had brought all of this stuff on himself. He wouldn't have gotten caught up in any of these things if he had not started using drugs himself. The drug use was the thing that had set everything in motion. From that point on, things just spiraled out of control. Billy had to get caught up in all of this drama to learn how to think of someone other than himself and had lost me in the process.... such a painful lesson to learn I thought.

I was not able to give Billy what he now wanted.... which was a second chance.... a chance to start over with me. And I knew that this was what he wanted and was trying to get around to asking me about. Our time had long since passed and I had gone on with my life.

I removed my hands from Billy's clasp, as I looked over at Steve and my children. Steve had a suggestive look on his face as if he were trying to tell me to let Billy know about the new life you have now. I smiled weakly, as I returned my attention back to Billy, who looked as if he was relieved to have everything off his chest.

"Billy…. I have to tell you something," I spoke steadily, searching his face for a reaction.

Billy watched me attentively, as I continued.

"We are no longer married. I have been remarried for over 5 years now."

Disappointment washed over Billy's face, as he hit the countertop with a closed fist. Compassion touched my heart as I placed a shaky hand over his fist.

Shaking his head, he turns back to face me, his eyes showing so much hurt. I was at a lost for words and my throat throbbed with stifled emotion.

"Your son Billy…. he's 10 years old. His name is Jamarr," my voice strained out.

"Would you like to meet him?"

Billy's mood appeared to lighten just a little as a half smile eased onto his face.

Looking over at Steve, I motioned for him to send Jamarr over to me. As Jamarr approached us, tears began to roll down Billy's cheeks. Holding Jamarr by the hand, I introduced him to Billy.

Billy was so overcome with emotion that he reached out and lifted Jamarr into his arms, hugging him tightly.

Sympathy for Billy tugged at my heart as I watched his emotional reunion with Jamarr. Leaning over and placing Jamarr back on the floor, Billy looks me square in the face with tear-filled eyes and asks -- "Does he know that I'm his father?"

I reached for Jamarr, who was now staring at Billy strangely and pulled him into my arms.

Sweetheart, go back over to Steve and your sister. Mom will be over to join you in a little while, okay?"

I kissed him on his cheek and sent him back to over to Steve.

Looking at Billy, I slowly nodded my head and with a strained voice said, "No, Jamarr doesn't know that you are his father."

"When will you tell him that I'm his father? Aren't you going to tell him?" Billy said, trying to gather his composure.

"I will tell him soon, since I know now that you are still among the living Billy."

Billy watched Jamarr as he walked back to table where Steve and Brianna were seated. Steve smiled proudly and waved back as Jamarr approached him.

"Is that your husband over there, Lynn," Billy asked reluctantly.

"Yes, it is," I replied. "And the little girl.... that's Brianna. She is my daughter and Steve's," I added.

I slid off the bar stool, smiling admirably at Steve and my two wonderful kids.

"Let me introduce you," I said, walking toward Steve and motioning for Billy to follow me.

Billy trailed reluctantly behind me, as I made my way over to Steve. Steve stood up from his chair, as we approached, adjusting his tie and eyeing Billy.

"Billy…. this is my husband Steve and my daughter Brianna," I said, radiantly displaying my love and admiration for my family.

Steve extended his hand to Billy's and he obliged likewise, as they shook hands strongly.

"It's been a long time Billy," Steve said. "Don't you remember me? I was from the Class of 73 at Whitmore High. Just about everyone called me the *Steve the Nerd* back then."

"Now I remember you. I think that you had a crush on Lynn back then, but I wasn't worried because I knew that she loved me. Wow man…. you have really changed a lot from back when we were in school. I would have never guessed that it was you."

Billy looked over at Brianna, who was sitting there, looking up, and smiling at him.

"You have a very beautiful daughter there," Billy commented, motioning toward Brianna. "You are a lucky man to have two such precious gems."

Steve's chest seemed to swell with pride at Billy's comment. He was very proud of his family and wasn't afraid to show it.

"Hey man, I think that I'm the lucky one," Steve said, as he flashed me a loving glance.

"Billy and I shouldn't be much longer honey, okay?" I said to Steve.

"It was nice seeing you again Billy," Steve said, while seating himself back in the chair.

I bent down and kissed Jamarr and Brianna's angelic faces, as they both looked up at me.

"Mom will be right back…. Mom loves you."

"I love you too, Mommy," they both chimed.

Billy and I walked back to the bar and seated ourselves on the bar stools. As I looked at Billy now, I would have never thought that I would love anyone other than him. Now, I have two beautiful children and a man who adores me. The life that I have right now is like a dream-come-true.

Billy cleared his throat and looked at me very strangely.

"Lynnie…. you know…. I still love you. I really thought that I would have had a chance to make things up to you. I know that you didn't deserve the treatment that you got, but I wanted a chance to be the man you deserve. When I was in prison, I went through drug rehabilitation. I'm clean now and I won't ever go back to drugs. All I wanted was the life that I had with you. I…. I still love you Lynnie. I want to help raise our son and be a good father to him. I'll never hurt you again…. I can promise you that Lynn, honey."

Billy's voice broke, as he lowered his head sobbing profusely. I realized that he was in pain, yet I knew that

I could not ease it in the way that he wanted. I wasn't in love with him anymore and I had a new life. I knew that what I was about to tell Billy would hurt him even more, but I had to be honest with him. My throat ached, as I tried to stifle the emotions that stirred deep within me. I closed my eyes, and took a deep breath before I spoke.

I lifted Billy's head gently, so that I could look him in the eyes as I spoke to him.

"Billy…. I know that you are in pain and I wish that I could take the pain away, but I can't. The life that we had together is gone now. I have a new husband…. a new life…. and two, precious children that I love more than life itself. I'm so very proud that you went through drug rehab and cleaned yourself up. I'm also grateful to you for not getting me involved in your drug dealings. You actually did an unselfish thing when you kept quiet about everything and went to prison. You protected your unborn child and me from the possibility of getting seriously injured or killed even. For that selfless act Billy, I will always be thankful and indebted to you. I love you as my son's father, but I'm in love with Steve…. he is my husband and my second chance at happiness. You have a second chance too now Billy…. to be happy and make a new life for yourself. You are already off to a great start by taking responsibility for your own actions, and by learning to not be selfish. As for your son …. Well, you will be able to see him whenever you want if you really want a chance to build a relationship with him, provided that you stay clean."

Tears began teasing the corners of my eyes, as I paused to contain my emotions. My speech had become stressed, yet I had to finish speaking what was on my mind and heart.

"I wish you the very best Billy," I said weakly. "Just stay on the road that you're on right now and everything will work out. I have to go now. Take care of yourself Billy, okay?"

As I turned to walk away, Billy called after me painfully. I turned and faced him momentarily.

"Take care of yourself Billy."

Billy watched sadly as I turned and walked away and out of his life. But my family was waiting for me. I was finally able to put what was once an unresolved conflict in my past to rest for good. Now, I could resume my new life with peace of mind and renewed faith…. thankful that I was granted a second chance at happiness.

* * * * * * * *

This Saturday morning when I awakened, I felt as though I had been somewhat reborn. I had finally gotten a chance to get all of the things I had held inside about Billy's abandoning me off my chest. I really did feel badly for him, but I also knew that there was nothing I could do to help him. His life was his own as was mine.

I put on some coffee and decided to watch the early morning news. I was totally shocked by what I heard the news spokesman say. I watched the T.V. in horror and disbelief as the spokesman was speaking of a tragic accident.

Last night there was a horrific, one vehicle crash just outside of the city limits of Charleston. The driver of the car had lost control of the car. The car hit a culvert and had overturned several times, throwing the driver from the vehicle. The vehicle came to rest on its' top several 100 yards from where it had hit the culvert. The victim has been identified as William Matthews and he was pronounced dead at the scene. The police at the scene felt that alcohol played a role in the accident because the victim smelled of alcohol and some broken bottles of liquor was found in the car. The police said that the coroner would definitely be able to rule whether or not the accident was alcohol-related in his report.

My blood seemed to run cold and tears welled in my eyes; I thought of the conversation I had with Billy yesterday evening. Billy must have started drinking heavily after I left him I told myself.

Guilt was trying to consume me, but I wouldn't allow it. *Lynnie -- it's not your fault. You did not cause this accident. You didn't force that liquor down Billy's throat. Feel sympathy and compassion if you want, as long as you are not blaming yourself for his death. It's not your fault. He did this my conscious advised me.* After taking some deep breaths, I began to calm down. It was true that Billy was upset about what I had said to him, but I didn't make him do this to himself. He just couldn't handle the fact that I had gone on with my life without him.

I really didn't want Billy out of my life this way, but I guess this was his fate. I most definitely refuse to blame myself for his unfortunate accident. He was responsible for his own actions just as I'm responsible for mine.

I do have a small regret…. that my son would not have a chance to get to know his biological father. Billy and I had our differences, but I would not have prevented him from trying to establish a relationship with his son. I will miss him.

Since Billy really was gone now, Steve asked if he could legally adopt Jamarr. He said that he would have never asked about adoption if Billy had survived. Steve wanted Jamarr to have the security and stability of having a real father, especially since he never got a chance to know his real father and that he has been the only father he has known. I agreed wholeheartedly with his suggestion because I knew that Steve loved my son very much and he simply couldn't ask for a better father.

When I reflect back to the pain and sadness I'd experienced in my past, my mind and heart will hold them as growth experiences and stepping-stones. My mother used to say that what didn't kill you, made you strong. Well, I have my own personal life experiences to relate to from which life has taught me. Life has an uncanny way of helping you to remember important lessons. The key is being able to forgive those who hurt you and in forgiving yourself. Forgive ourselves for at times having chosen darkness over light, hatred over love, and fear over faith. Some say that when we make mistakes, those mistakes make us evil. That is not true! We simply have temporarily forgotten the truth of who we are. We are still Children of God no matter what we have done in the past. As Jesus said to Mary Magdalene, "Your sins have been forgiven. Go and sin no more!" We must take this same attitude with ourselves... and with the people in our lives. We must learn to love and accept ourselves completely — both in our perfection and our foibles. We need to forgive ourselves. We need to realize that we will make mistakes at times, and that these mistakes are part of the learning process. Have compassion for yourself and do not judge yourself harshly for making mistakes. Acknowledge the truth of who you are. Loving yourself means acknowledging who you are, where you've been, and where you are going. It seems that you cannot really come to appreciate what you have until you lose it or no longer have it in your possession. But I was blessed with a second chance and I will take full advantage of it.

9 781957 895062